Sober Faith

STEPHANIE PERRY MOORE

The Negro National Anthem

Lift every voice and sing
Till earth and heaven ring,
Ring with the harmonies of Liberty;
Let our rejoicing rise
High as the listening skies,
Let it resound loud as the rolling sea.
Sing a song, full of the faith that the dark past has taught us,
Sing a song, full of the hope that the present has brought us,
Facing the rising sun, of our new day begun
Let us march on till victory is won.

So begins the Black National Anthem, by James Weldon Johnson in 1900. Lift Every Voice is the name of the joint imprint of The Institute for Black Family Development and Moody Publishers, a division of the Moody Bible Institute.

Our vision is to advance the cause of Christ through publishing African-American Christians who educate, edify, and disciple Christians in the church community through quality books written for African-Americans.

The Institute for Black Family Development is a national Christian organization. It offers degreed and non-degreed training nationally and internationally to established and emerging leaders from churches and Christian organizations. To learn more about The Institute for Black Family Development, write us at:

The Institute for Black Family Development
15151 Faust
Detroit, MI 48223

Since 1984, Moody Publishers has been dedicated to equip and motivate people to advance the cause of Christ by publishing evangelical Christian literature and other media for all ages, around the world. Because we are a ministry of the Moody Bible Institute of Chicago, a portion of the proceeds from the sale of this book go to train the next generation of Christian leaders.

Moody Publishers
c/o Moody Publishers Ministries
820 N. LaSalle Blvd.
Chicago, IL 60610

Sober Faith

STEPHANIE PERRY MOORE

Moody Press   'Lift Every Voice'

Library of Congress Cataloging-in-Publication Data is
available.

ISBN: 0-8024-4237-4

7 9 10 8
Printed in the United States of America

For
Charles
(1967–1998)

my special
high school friend

FAITH
tells me I'll
see you in
Heaven.

Contents

Acknowledgments 9

1. Toasting Into Trouble 11

2. Hosting Without Permission 22

3. Suffering the Consequences 30

4. Traveling to Love 40

5. Modeling Without Poise 51

6. Discipling My Life 57

7. 'Tempting to Die 68

8. Crashing Downhill 74

9. Waiting with Expectation 81

10. Acting for Him 91

11. Facing My Fears 97

12. Agreeing to Disagree 104

13. Hiding the Truth 114

14. Exempting Your Test 122

15. Walking with Grace 131

Acknowledgments

As it says in 2 Peter 1:5–8, there are several qualities that every Christian must possess to keep from being ineffective and unproductive in the knowledge of our Lord Jesus Christ. In comparison, there are several people who keep me together so that I can always be a productive and effective Christian novelist. Thanks to all of you for helping me write and maintain *Sober Faith*.

To my reading pool, Sierra Hunter, Kimmie Johnson, Launi Perriman, Cole Smith, and Trace Williams, and to my assistant, Tiffany Austin: You all show me *GOODNESS*. The way you give freely of your time and talents is a blessing that makes this book the best it can be. Thanks for answering the call and making my project your own. Your involvement gives me the faith to believe people will get the book's message.

To the imprint, *Lift Every Voice,* and to my publisher, Moody Press: You all provide *KNOWLEDGE.* By helping me put this work on the shelves, together we are showing teenagers how to please God in their daily lives. Thanks for empowering my words with substance. Your direction gives me the faith to know that this book will be distributed God's way.

To my parents, Franklin and Shirley Perry: You both taught me *SELF-CONTROL.* Looking within and liking what I see comes from good upbringing. Thanks for encouraging me to use my God-given talents. Your support gives me the faith to realize God wants to use . . . even me.

To my daughters, Sydni and Sheldyn: You two lil' angels give me *PERSERVERANCE.* The will to succeed is real for me because I long to make you proud. Thanks for the teddy bear hugs and the butterfly kisses that enable me to keep writing, even when I'm tired. Your innocence gives me the faith to comprehend the unconditional love we receive from our heavenly Father.

To my spiritual mentor, Karen Loritts, and my discipleship partners, Marla Clark and Shawn Mitchell: You all help me aim for *GODLINESS*. Keeping focused on God's Word helps to make me a better writer. Thanks for urging me not to fall short in my Christian walk. Your influence gives me faith to know that I, too, can please God.

To the reader, wherever you are: You help me display *BROTHERLY KINDNESS*. Each word in this novel was meant to build you up. Thanks for letting your hearts be challenged to live for God. Your unknown situations give me the faith to believe God will answer your prayers.

To my husband, Derrick Moore: You give me *LOVE*. Every day of mine is a day of joy because you are in it. Thanks for standing by me, even when I make it hard to be near. Your protection gives me the faith to see why God made you the head.

And to Jesus Christ: You are *LIFE!* You are goodness, knowledge, self-control, perserverance, godliness, brotherly kindness, and love. Thanks for loving me enough to give me eternal life. Your sacrifice gives me faith to know my living is not in vain!

1

Toasting Into Trouble

"*P*ayton Skky, you're the most beautiful girl I've ever laid eyes on," my boyfriend genuinely whispered in my ear, as we waltzed across the ballroom in high style.

Leaning my head on his strong shoulder, I quickly replied, "I don't know how I look on the outside, but on the inside being in your arms makes me feel like Cinderella."

Continuing to twirl, I reflected on why I was so happy now, and how the last several months had been more trying than any other period of my short seventeen years. I'd been through quite a bit. Yet, as I trusted God to straighten out my problems, life had gotten remarkably better.

See, I used to date a guy named Dakari Graham. That's Kari 'The Bomb' Graham. This guy is drop-dead fine: caramel skin, perfect flashing smile, and an 'all that' personality. If you didn't know better, you'd think he was Denzel Washington's little brother. Boy, is he smooth.

Anyway, we were together for two great but crazy years. On again, off again—better, best, and sometimes worst. Even though things weren't perfect, I still thought we'd get married one day. You know, high school sweethearts graduating into eventual wedded bliss.

Sounds great, BUT, Dakari had a different agenda. To be blunt, he broke up with me because I wouldn't put out. He found someone else to give him what I wouldn't. Honestly, it hurt badly that Dakari would rather have none of me if he couldn't have one particular thing. It took a long time, too, for me to see that. I had to get past all the fluff to see that Mr. Graham was missing one particular characteristic. In all his beauty, he failed to hold a strong love for the Lord as deeply in his heart as he held his ego. Luckily, before it was too late, I learned that it's better to please God than to please a guy.

After struggling and straining to stay pure, both physically and spiritually, I chose the higher ground and walked away. What a great choice.

"What are you thinking so hard about, pretty lady?" my escort inquired.

"Oh, nothing," I replied. "I'm just so blessed to be here with you."

When I trusted my heavenly Father and dwelt in His goodness, the Lord soothed my aching heart. He helped me turn my focus back squarely toward Him. See, God knew better than I that I needed much more in my life than just a cute guy. He knew I needed to firmly trust Him in my love life, my friendships, everything. After I got the lesson, the Lord sent my way one of His own to call my own. Mr. Tad Taylor and I have only been dating for a few months, but he's a strong, godly guy. Plus, he's tall, dark, and handsome. That doesn't hurt either.

Although staying pure 'til marriage will be tough, with Tad there's no pressure. We both have the same goal. He actually has a deep relationship with the Lord, which helps him stay strong. That relationship means more to him than anything he could get from me. He's so much unlike my former beau, Mister "I-want-it, I-get-it," who only cared about satisfying his flesh.

The music was bold, yet sweet. The moment was precious and priceless. The ballroom was strikingly elegant, decked out in red, white, and gold floral. Mom and her Link sisters had really outdone themselves putting this affair together. As Tad and I moved in rhythm with the other dancers, I took it all in and silently reminded myself to tell Mom, "Thanks."

Glancing out of the corner of my eye, I saw my three girlfriends: Rain, Lynzi, and Dymond. We had a sisterhood that meant more to me than a million-dollar savings bond. We were all different, yet genuinely enjoyed each other.

We'd just gone through a terrible misunderstanding—the kind that happens when you make assumptions and jump to conclusions without getting the facts. Fortunately, God allowed us to not be deceived with foolish lies. Thus, we straightened things out and vowed to remain close forever. This Debutante Ball was so special because all of us were overjoyed that our friendship was back intact.

Of the three, I'm the closest to Rain. We've been buddies since we were tots. Rain is my confidante and I'm hers. There's nothing we can't talk about. Although sometimes we don't agree, there's never a time we won't hear each other out. We try to tell each other the truth—the real, hard truth.

As I glanced at the gorgeous, tall, slender girl nearby, I couldn't believe our time on the same road was fading out towards different paths. She was dancing with her equally tall beau, Tyson, who didn't go to our school, Lucy Laney. He went to one of our rival schools, T.W. Josey.

Then there was Lynzi. Boy, had the two of us gone through a lot lately! Both of us had had boyfriend problems. Not only are there biblical reasons not to have sex before you are married, but Lynzi found out there could be terrible consequences to that sin as well. My girl had a close call; she thought she was pregnant. By grace, only grace, she was not. Luckily, things are looking up for her too, although she is back with her all too pushy guy, Bam. Supposedly, she's got a different mind-set this time. She's trying not to make the same mistake again. I hope she succeeds.

And Dymond, how gorgeous she is as she turns. To think people used to call her fat. Yeah, she's chunky, but boy is she fly. Her thick-framed boyfriend Fatz is crazy, fun, and cool.

My parents seemed so proud sitting nearby as they gazed at me. My mom wanted me to be a deb for years. She is a member of The Links organization, who sponsors this event. At first, I didn't think I'd like being a debutante, but I have truly enjoyed the experience.

Being a deb is as precious as being a budding rose, blooming and blossoming in your own time. We young ladies are learning to make the most out of every day and trying to spring forth goodness. Yet, even as we change, we hope to change into something better.

As we did the figure eight dance and changed partners, I was paired with my ex-boyfriend. He is a senior, just like me, at the same high school. He told me he was going to back down from coming on so strong, but as I noticed him caressing my back and drawing me even closer to him, I kinda figured something else was up.

"What are you doing? What are you doing? Don't you realize it won't work for us anymore? You called it off at the beginning of the school year to date someone else. You didn't want me then, and I don't want you now," I breathed, full of emotion.

"Yeah, I hear what you say, but I also hear my heart. You just met that Tad dude, man. Ya'll only been together . . . what, a couple months? We were together for years, baby, for years, and you s'pose to be mine. I'm sorry, I just gotta let you know that when you want this, when you want what you used to have, it's yours," Dakari verbalized, as he spun me back into the arms of the one I wanted to be with.

"What was that all about? The brother seemed like he was sayin' some things I'd have a problem with," Tad voiced in an overprotective tone.

"It was nothing. Kari just made me realize that sometimes you don't know what you have until it's gone, and now that I have you I don't want to make Dakari's mistake. So let's not waste time talking about him. Let's continue enjoying this magical moment, 'cause I can't imagine anything going wrong. Our proms are coming up, and pretty soon we'll be graduating, then summer, then college. And I'm ready for it all!" I said to him excitedly.

Tad then flung me back into the arms of Dakari once again. I hated to leave his embrace, but I knew we'd be apart for only a brief moment. My eyes, however, couldn't focus in on my present dance partner. They lingered on the one who owned my heart.

"Why you keep staring at the brother?" Dakari voiced with jealousy. "Him and Starr are all the way on the other side of the room. You got the best-lookin' dude in the place right here. So, check me out!"

I teased, "Someone wants my attention . . . how precious."

Waltzing with Dakari wasn't so terrible. Actually, we were laughing at some of everything. I was glad that he seemed to be cool with us being friends. That's the only way it would ever be.

"Stop, stop putting your hands all over me!" I heard coming from across the room.

The most physically attractive girl at the ball was acting as if she'd lost her mind. And the scariest part about it to me, as I stared at her pushing away from the guy she was twirling with, was that it was Tad Taylor. My escort. Although the orchestra kept playing the music, we all stopped dancing.

Forty-nine debs and forty-nine escorts all turned inwardly to view the spectacle before us.

Starr's long, black, shiny hair was swishing back and forth, as she was pointing at Tad in the weirdest way. He, on the other hand, kept his poise and tried to calm her down. "What are you talking about? Touch you? We're just dancing," he retorted.

"D-d-don't you try . . . d-d-don't you even act like you weren't trying to get this," Starr mumbled, stuttering and falling all at once.

Dakari got over there just in time to catch her before she fell to the floor. No one knew what was up. We all were so scared. Her parents, Mr. and Mrs. Love, rushed on to the floor.

Before they could get to her Dakari yelled, "She's OK, she's OK. She just passed out."

His words calmed everyone down. At least she hadn't died right there before us. And then Dakari explained, "She's drunk."

I rushed to Tad's side. "Oh my gosh, what's going on?" I said to him.

"Yo' boy's right. She kept tripping over me. Out of nowhere she started accusing me of stuff. Then she just passed out. But I smelled something on her breath and asked her if she was OK."

She's drunk. Inebriated. Intoxicated. How could someone pour down so much alcohol that they would pass out? She had to be totally out of her mind to drink so much. She had been humiliated earlier in the evening when this guy from the crowd called her some horrible names; maybe it had been too much for her to take.

Dakari and Mr. Love carried Starr off to the side. As she slowly came to, her sluggish body wasn't its usual together self. It was weird to witness.

Amazingly, the music hadn't stopped. However, no one

felt like dancing, most of all Tad. Even though it was a lie, the accusations still hurt.

Velda Flannery, the choreographer, started pushing everyone to get in line for the last dance, The Promenade March. We were to march and parade ourselves before the crowd one last time and then march out into the lobby. As the group began the dance, the pep in our step was lost. Even though I was in a daze over the whole thing myself, I turned to Tad to help him regain his zeal for the moves.

"It's OK. Everybody knows she was making it up, Tad. Try to forget it," I urged.

"No, it doesn't have anything to do with what she said," Tad told me.

He was very frustrated. I hated the fact that something was weighing heavy on his mind. I hoped he'd open up.

"People don't ever think about it . . . consequences . . . actions. I wish folks would think about stuff. Then . . ." Tad counseled the air.

He was so disgusted that he couldn't even finish his thought. Although he never regained his enthusiasm, we finished the dance. I was so thankful that he was my escort. As we marched out of the place, I thought, though it wasn't a perfect night, Tad was surely a perfect date.

About thirty minutes had passed. Everyone stood in line to take pictures with their escorts under the display of roses. Even though the fizzle had faded from our evening like a soda turns flat, Tad and I managed to pose with a smile.

"Are you ready? I'm kinda ready to go," Tad said to me after our shots were finished.

"No, no, we can't go now. They're . . . um . . . having refreshments for us in the back room. Just hang with me for a few more minutes. Please?" I begged him with puppy dog eyes, trying to convince him to stay.

17

Tad agreed to stay. When we entered the other room, he went to stand with my girlfriends' escorts, Tyson, Bam, and Fatz. I sat down with my girls, and we reviewed the night's events.

"Miss Starr had two episodes tonight, ya'll. See, ya trip on folks and that stuff comes back to you," Dymond giggled.

"'Ya'll'! What kinda word is that? With the GPA you have and all the stuff you've got going for you, you talk so crazy, Dy," I said, actually trying to stop the gossip.

My three friends looked at me as if I was the one who was crazy. Slang is all we ever speak to each other. It's our own language. It's who we are. How we breathe.

I sounded like my mother. "OK, OK, OK, I'm trippin'," I apologized.

They all shook their heads in agreement and we laughed. The detour had worked. At least we weren't still bashing Starr. I was kinda angry too. I figured she had enough to deal with without us trippin'. Suddenly, we all felt a chill and simultaneously turned our heads toward the door.

"I kinda feel sorry for her," I said to my three girlfriends.

Starr was standing there in front of all of her peers. She had to be embarrassed. She had to be humiliated. Dakari was nowhere around.

"Who's she lookin' for?" Rain questioned.

"Don't know, but I saw Dakari leave. He's through with that girl. And needs to be," Lynzi said.

"Why do you feel sorry for her anyway, Payton?" Dymond asked. "Who cares about her? All the drama she gave you, taking yo' man and stuff. Tryin' to get your other one. And you feel sorry for her. Tuhh! Give me a break."

I couldn't answer them. Starr had made my senior year crazy. To a rational person, it did seem kinda stupid for me to care about her feelings and to care about her pain so much. But I did care. I cared a lot. We were about to graduate in a few months. Prom was before us, and our summer was full of expectations. Then college right down the road. Yet, I couldn't feel completely happy when someone else was sad.

I left my friends to go to Starr's side. Before I could get there, Starr started towards Tad. "OK, OK, what's going on?" I said to myself. "What is she saying to him?" Tad saw me and reached his hand out to mine. I came over to his side.

Strangely enough, Starr unexpectedly replied with remorse, "I owe you both an apology. Um, I'm sorry. I feel sick now and I know I made a fool of myself, but I didn't have to say what Dakari said I said to you. I actually can't even remember too much, but . . . I just want to tell you that I'm sorry."

"You should be sorry, you lush!" was yelled out from some unknown, cruel person in the room.

Whoever said that terrible remark should have been thrown out. However, the sponsors weren't around yet. Plus, no one knew who said it.

Starr picked up the bottom of her dress and left the premises. Although once again I felt bad for her, I knew I couldn't solve all her problems. So, I did the only thing anyone could do to help her. I silently prayed.

"Lord, she needs You," I breathed at heaven. "Starr Love needs Your help."

"Let's go!" Bam came behind Tad and me and whispered. "I got a surprise for ya'll in my ride. C'mon, c'mon, c'mon!"

After gathering the group, all of us were finally out at Bam's car. He went to the trunk and pulled out a bottle. At first, I didn't know what to make of the situation.

"Man, what's up?" Tad asked.

"Ahh, just a little som'n, som'n to celebrate this wonder-

19

ful accomplishment. You know, the coming out of these fo' beautiful ladies."

Bam started passing cups around. Dymond and Lynzi grabbed theirs instantly. Rain hesitated, but then slowly took a cup herself. Like a heart in two pieces, I was torn. Tad gently leaned over to me and uttered, "I don't want any part of this. Let's go."

My girlfriends looked at me and could sense my reluctance. I almost felt as if they were in my ear and heard every private word Tad spoke to me. Though it wasn't a cool evening, the confrontation chilled me.

Tad didn't wait around for my decision. He left me standing with the group. His dark frame, usually so upbeat, now took on a somber appearance. Watching him stroll away, I sensed his disappointment.

As Tad walked away Bam blurted, "Man, don't be no punk. It ain't nothin' but a lil' sip. What's up? Ya can't handle that?"

"Man . . . whatever," Tad retorted, turned, and retreated. "Not that I owe you any explanation, but I don't touch the sauce. My Bible tells me not to. Havin' God's approval is more important than yours."

"Alright then, church boy. I hear ya. Hope ya don't mind if I have a lil' nip-nip?" Bam kiddingly questioned.

With a serious expression, Tad replied, "Sad scene, brother, if your 'little' turns into a lot. Then the next thing you know, you and this car end up in a ditch somewhere."

Surely he was exaggerating. What could it really hurt? I thought. I mean it was really only just a few sips. Nothing more! I wasn't going to drink the whole bottle. Besides, I had never tried alcohol. I was curious.

I knew Lynzi dabbled with it. Her mom let her drink wine at home. She had been trying to get me to taste it for a while. I wasn't interested in doing so, 'til that moment.

As I watched Bam pour my glass, I had some doubts.

Although I knew I shouldn't, I really wanted to. That desire to be daring grew stronger as I heard the sizzle fill my cup.

"Are you ready?" Tad probed, as he returned and nudged my shoulder.

Firmly, I replied, "No, I want to try it."

Disgusted with me, he stormed away. As I slowly lifted my glass, I reassured myself that I did want to do this. Life was changing for me. So many good things were happening. I deserved a celebration. "Cheers," Bam toasted.

Before the alcoholic beverage could touch my tongue, I witnessed my boyfriend kick his car door. Doing what I wanted was causing us problems. The thought of losing him over champagne made me begin to taste how bitterly stupid that choice might prove to be.

Suddenly I shook from the strong taste. Then questions filled what was left of my brain, as my heart felt warm. I realized I might have been in over my head. Was this the right choice? Was one drink, one drink too many? Was I toasting into trouble?

2

Hosting
Without Permission

Seconds after the funny fizzle went into my system, I felt a little woozy. It was weird, but it wasn't totally a bad weird. I actually liked it. So I smiled, and my peers knew I wasn't against the taste.

Lynzi bumped me. Dymond gave me a high-five. Rain simply giggled. I could tell she was a little woozy, too.

"You know you like it. Yeah, all ya'll like it," Bam said with such confidence. "Well, folks coming out of the ball now. We . . . we need to . . . we need to move this joint. What's up? Where we goin', where we goin', where we goin', ladies?"

"Ah, let's go over to Payton's house. Her parents are gon' be at the Links' after-party thing for a while, right? Right, Payton? We're coming to your house," Lynzi invited herself.

Without really thinking about my parents, my date, or if I even wanted company, I said, "Sure, whatever."

Bam tried to pour me another glass. I glanced at Tad, and the car door he just bashed in, and refused. Walking over to him, I knew he was angry. His negative response kinda bothered me. Why be so tight and stiff? Why be so against fun? Why trip?

"It's not that serious, really it's not," I mumbled to myself. And just when I thought it wasn't that bad, I tripped over my own feet. My dress hit the concrete. Mud and water splashed on me. I knew the white gown was ruined, along with my pride.

The mean stare melted from Tad's face as he dashed over to me and helped me up. The gentleman he has always been since the first day I've known him came flying out like a Lear jet. I loved how much he cared for me.

"You OK?" he asked me softly.

"Yeah, but look at me. I'm a mess."

He could've said I told you so. He could've said it was the alcohol. He could've said so many things. Luckily, he said nothing.

"I think my . . . my foot is sprained. It hurts—ouch!" I told him as he gently touched it. Then I walked a couple of steps. Although it hurt, I could walk. My so-called friends were laughing! As if this was funny. My mom would surely kill me for ruining my outfit.

My mother was planning to send it to Pillar, my estranged cousin on my father's side who lives in Denver, Colorado. See, her crazy father, my dad's older brother, said he wasn't buying a prom gown 'til she was a senior. If she planned to go she'd have to get a dress from somewhere else. Being that Pillar is my mother's goddaughter, they have remained in touch. My mother agreed to help her. Help her with my stuff. So even though Pillar doesn't like me, she was supposed to wear MY gown at her junior prom.

Did I bring this on myself? Did I trip from drinking only one drink? Or did I fall because I had too much pride to stand up to Tad for what I believed was OK? This adventurous night was filled with questions.

We'd been riding for twenty minutes. My ankle was feeling a little better. After driving in complete silence, my guy spoke.

Curiously, Tad asked, "Are they following us? I see Bam's car right on my tail, and two other cars behind them. What's going on? Why are they turning into your neighborhood?"

"Well, you know, Rain lives around here also. But, um . . ." I paused trying to get out of it. "But, um . . . they're coming to my house."

Tad's relaxed disposition changed instantly. I knew this was going to be uncomfortable for him. Unfortunately, I had already said they could come.

"I'll just pull in your driveway and see to it that you get inside. I don't want to get in the way of the party," Tad informed me with sarcasm.

"Don't be like that. Please, please, please just stay for a minute. I mean . . . uh, we had such a great night. I don't want it to end like this. Don't be mad. I . . . I . . . I know I should have asked you," my batting eyes and soft voice uttered to him. "I'm sorry, but—don't go."

Tad decided to stay. He wasn't that comfortable being in the midst of all my friends, yet he was as great a sport as he was on the football field. I came up to him several times just to make sure he was OK. He assured me he was fine. However, I knew if he could have had things his way, we'd have been alone right now. Not to mess around, just to kind of be on the same page, and although I didn't take another drink, Bam, Lynzi, Fatz, and Dymond were on their third bottle.

Bam left my crib to go and get something. "Chill out," said Lynzi when I asked what it was. I had a bad feeling about where this evening was going. Although my folks were not home and my brother, Perry, was sleeping over with a friend, I still didn't want my house trashed. I also didn't want company 'til crazy hours of the morning. Church was tomorrow, and no matter how tired I was from the ball, I knew my parents were going to make me go to Sunday school.

Asking an irritated Tad nicely, I voiced, "So where do you think Bam's gone?"

"I'm sure he went to get some more to drink. Champagne is probably not strong enough for him."

"He can't bring anything in my house. I can't have any cups or anything like that laying around. My parents will know. They'll be able to notice somethin' was up. I'll get in trouble. No way!" I panicked.

"I don't mean any harm, Payton, but . . . umm, you don't want it in your house only because you might get in trouble," my guy probed. "They've already poured down a bunch of alcohol. If they drink any more, they should not be on the road. Nobody should leave here 'til they at least sober up. Have you thought about that?"

What he had preached earlier was coming true. It was unfortunate, but the 'one drink' had turned into way too many. And however awkward the confrontation with my so-called friends would be, I couldn't allow any of it in my house.

I looked around to find Rain. I didn't see her. Surely she hadn't gone upstairs. Tyson, Mr. Basketball Star, was bouncing from room to room. I searched every room upstairs—mine, my brother's, the two guest rooms, even the three baths. After all that looking, I still didn't find my best friend and her escort. Then I heard commotion coming from the double doors of my parents' room, on the main floor of the house. Rain surely knew not to go in there, I thought. I thought wrong.

I heard screaming and yelling. Rushing downstairs, I

tried not to reinjure my ankle. I opened my parents' oak bedroom doors and practically stepped into the Jerry Springer show. Lynzi and Rain were going at it.

Apparently, after I sorted through all the drama, Rain had gone into my parents' bath and came out to find Lynzi with Tyson on the bed. Their clothes were on and they hadn't started kissing, but the position was totally compromising. I, too, was disgusted with Lynzi.

Tipsy or not, she surely knew Tyson wasn't her man. Yet, it was as if she didn't care. Although Rain was strong, I have never seen her violent, but she flew out of that bathroom and pushed Lynzi two feet back.

"Oh, it's like that, huh? What? You want some of this? You want to push me?" Lynzi huffed as she tried to gather her composure and confront Rain.

Rain cried hysterically, "Tyson, how could you? I know she's tacky, but how could you let her in your arms?"

"Baby, she came on to me," he explained.

Before Tyson could finish explaining, Lynzi and Rain started cat fighting. It was so ridiculous. So petty. So unnecessary. And the culprit was the alcohol.

Tad knew that instantly. I, on the other hand, didn't see it so plainly. I just figured Lynzi was being flirtatious Lynzi, and hurt her dear friend in the process.

After the uproar, Lynzi came out with a bloody nose and Rain a bruised arm. Even worse than that, they broke my mom's vase. Just great. Just great.

"What've you guys done?" I yelled when I saw the pieces scattered on the floor. "Which one of ya'll got two thousand dollars? My mom bought this crazy thing years ago, in Paris. Perry and I have always been scared of breaking it. To us it was priceless; now look at this. It's . . . it's ruined!"

Tyson ignorantly suggested, "Can't you just glue the thing back together?"

I stormed out of the room in frustration. As soon as I left

their presence, the front door to my home opened. Bam entered the hallway with two cases of beer.

"Oh no, I don't think so," I said to him, while pushing him back out the front door. But he wouldn't budge, even as I kept pushing. As I tried to nudge him once more, my ears were irritated by the thundering sound from the living room.

Dymond and Fatz were playing some filthy rap song that they had pulled from her vehicle. They didn't even ask; they just assumed I wanted to hear it. As loud as they were playing it, the whole neighborhood could have heard it. And when I went to turn it down, they both looked at me as if I were crazy. Dymond danced around me to the beat playing in her own head and turned the stereo back up.

"C'mon girl, listen and groove," she said, taking my hands and making me move with her. "Girl, your man's in there in the family room all by himself. You need to loosen up so he'll loosen up and have some fun. Don't be so serious."

"Don't be so serious? You don't even know what just happened! Lynzi and Rain are in my parents' room not only breaking things up, but beating each other up as well. You guys are out here acting like lunatics, like you've lost your minds. I see my mom's good pillows thrown all crazy in the living room. Ya'll had to be dancing on the couch or doing something. Bam got more alcohol and brought it into in my parents' house. You know I'm not supposed to be drinking, much less have company over here drinking in the house," I said, basically talking to myself, because my friend was dancing, not listening.

I thought things couldn't get any crazier. Ten minutes later, they did. Bam and Fatz had beer cans in quite a few places. Chips were all around the formal area of my house. Fingerprint smears were all over the glass tables.

I went to the bathroom for a minute of peace and I just

prayed, "Lord, I don't know how I got myself into this mess. How wanting to celebrate turned into such a crazy night is beside me. I honestly didn't think it was wrong and I can't even tell You that I now believe it was . . . at least my part anyway. However, my stupid friends are taking it to the extreme. I'm sorry, but I'm sure You agree. They're pretty dumb, drinking and driving. I don't even know how to make coffee. I can't let them drive. My parents will be home in a second. Oh Lord, I'm sorry, but I do need Your help."

After coming out of my solace, I thought of Tad. He had to be able to help me. Surely he could. He was the only person in the house who had been rational all night long. Yeah, he had to be able to help me.

"Tad, where are you going?" I called out as I saw him at the front door about to leave.

He explained, "Just not my kind of scene, Payton. I think you need to decide what's important to you and what you want to be around. This just isn't me. I got this out of the car for you."

He handed me a box. I was in awe when I witnessed the gorgeous gold cross and chain.

On the entry stand was a dozen red roses. I went over to them and admired the beautiful arrangement. The card read, "Thanks for giving me the honor of escorting the most lovely debutante of all. Tad."

" The necklace is so pretty, and the flowers smell beautiful," I uttered with sweet emotion. "This means more than you'll ever know."

Tad had the beer box in his hand. There was also a can by his foot. He knelt down and picked it up.

As he stood loaded down with cans, he told me, "I'm going to take this to my car and dump it somewhere so your parents won't see this all over the house. You know I care about you a lot and I don't want you to get in trouble. Seeing you in this environment tonight . . . I just don't know if you're for me."

My lips moved to say "Sorry," yet I couldn't utter a word. My heart was breaking. He was fed up. I had chosen others over him, and for what? Trouble, problems, a party? How crazy of me.

No sooner than he could open the door, it opened from the other side. No, I thought. No, it can't be.

"Mom! Dad!" I said surprised and scared.

The look on their faces told me more than they could ever say. Seeing our lovely home trashed out made them very, very angry.

"Tad, what are you doing with beer?" my mom quizzed in a disappointed tone.

"Young man, don't ever come back here!" my dad said without waiting for mom's question to be answered.

"But, Dad, you don't underst—" I hopelessly tried explaining.

Dad demanded in haste, "Payton Skky, you get up to your room; I'll get all these people out of here!"

"Sir, if I could just explain," Tad tried saying.

"Son, I trusted you with my daughter. I don't want to hear anything you have to say," the stern voice of my daddy replied.

It was as if all my friends sensed my parents' existence in the home. They all flocked to the door and exited out. Endless tears rolled down my face.

After everyone was gone and the door was shut, my mom looked at me and said, "I can't believe you'd betray our trust like this. What were you thinking, young lady, hosting without permission?"

3

Suffering
the Consequences

om, where's my phone?" I asked, kinda agitated, the next morning.

I had to call Tad. I had to talk to him. I had to explain why I let things get so out of control. Though I didn't know what I'd say, I had to try.

When I rolled over and reached for my phone that is usually positioned on the nightstand, it wasn't there. So, I knew my mother had come in and taken it sometime during the course of the night. I'm sure it was a part of my punishment, but I needed to tell her that I got the point. I'd learned my lesson. Now, I wanted my phone back.

Unfortunately, she wasn't trying to cater to my demands. Although in a few short months I'd be on my own anyway, I felt as if I were back in preschool. I was still being treated like a child by my parents.

I couldn't believe my father wrongly assumed that Tad was responsible for bringing the alcohol into the house. I so hoped it would be easy to clear all of this up. However, if not having a phone was any indication of the severity of my troubles, then I was on a rocky road.

"Payton Skky, don't come in here asking me any questions. And you know I don't appreciate the brash tone you're using with me. You are the one that crossed the line last night. Now, I hate to tell you, darling, but I have no clue when you'll receive your phone back. Oh . . . don't bother looking for your mobile. It's been taken as well. And you are to be in directly after school," my mom dictated.

Walking back to my room, I was angry. Actually, I was storming back to my room. That's how angry I was. My telephone! How could they take my telephone? I could see me having to stay inside, but goodness gracious. Why my phone? Surely I should be able to talk. It's not like I'm a kid. I'm a graduating senior. I'm due some respect. I'm going to be at parties next year anyway, and that's only a few months away.

Besides, I stayed up 'til four in the morning cleaning up the mess. The two-thousand-dollar vase was gonna be taken from my savings account. That was punishment enough! Shoot!

I used to be scared of leaving; now I couldn't wait to leave this place. I couldn't wait to be on my own. I couldn't wait to be independent.

After church service, later that day, Rain came up to me and tried to carry on a conversation. She acted as if nothing had happened the night before. Like we were cool, and everything was A-OK. I thought she was crazy. She must not have been the same girl that was over at my house last night, in my parents' room, causing a brawl and breaking valuables.

Whether Rain thought it was a big deal or not, it was a big deal to me. I couldn't just dismiss it. And I was never a fake friend. What I felt was what I gave off. No one ever had to wonder if I had a problem with them. They knew it, by my actions and by my words.

"Why won't you talk to me?" Rain said as she touched my arm, trying to turn me towards her. "You're a senior! You would think you wouldn't act like an elementary-age child. Stop ignoring me. Tell me what's up."

She stayed on me. She got in my face one too many times. Even though I was at church, I was about to lose it. My friends had gotten me in trouble, with my parents and with my guy. I was mad at all three of my girlfriends. Now it was time to let one of them hear my frustration.

"You know what, Rain? You think *I'm* acting like a child, huh? I really don't care what you think. If anyone was acting like a child last night, it was you. Children only care about their own feelings," I lashed out. "They care nothing about others. And what you did last night, in my parents' room, told me that you were the kid. Especially since you care nothing about destroying my parents' bedroom."

"Well, you know I didn't mean for all of that to happen," she said in a whining voice. "I'm mad at Lynzi—all over Ty like she thought he was Bam. I need you to help me set her straight. Please don't be mad at me. You know it was a big mistake. I need your help."

"I'm going through some stuff of my own, thanks to you guys. So, you just have to deal with your own problems. I can't hold your hand anymore. As you said, we are about to go to college. Grow up!" I lashed out, before I stormed out of church and got into my Jeep to drive home.

As I headed towards my place, I was relieved that my parents didn't take my vehicle, or at least they hadn't yet. My mother had given strict instructions to drive straight home. However, it was kinda hot. I wanted a soda badly. So, I stopped off at a corner store to get something to quench my thirst.

I was kinda glad I had to usher today. That let me come to church earlier than my family, drive my own car, and get to where I had to go without hearing any of that stuff my folks were talking about.

After purchasing a Coke, I walked back to my car. Tad Taylor was heavily on my mind, a ton of bricks crushing on my brain. How was I going to do it? How was I going to relieve the pressure? How was I going to explain all of this?

Suddenly out of nowhere, the pay phone that I'd seen many times before at the store's entrance came into view. The thought came, *Why don't you just call him?* I didn't have a cell phone, but I had just enough change in my hand to make the call.

Butterflies were flying around in my stomach. Since we hadn't been dating that long, I guess I was nervous as to how Tad would respond to our dilemma. Knowing that he usually goes to the early service at his church, I hoped he was home. Getting past the reluctance, my fingers did the dialing.

"Hi Mrs. Taylor, it's, umm, Payton. May I speak to Tad?"

"Well hey, sweetie! I hear you sure did look nice last night at that ball. You sure can speak to my son. Let me go get him. One second," his mother said in a sweet manner.

After taking what seemed like forever, my guy came to the phone. His voice didn't sound excited. It was as if he didn't want to be near me or have anything to do with me.

"Hey, you're just kinda sitting on the phone," I told him after a while of no conversation.

"You're not saying too much either. Anyway, I'm busy studying. I gotta go," Tad told me in a depressed tone.

My heart was breaking. I didn't know what to say, or how to reach out to him. It was killing me, too, since the guy I cared so much for was moving further and further away. I had hoped his anger would have gone away, but it hadn't gone anywhere. Apparently, it was still built up inside of him. His disappointment in me was making it hard for me to bear.

I thought, *Lord, is there something I can say to make the needed change? Is there something I can do to make him not be so angry? Fix this for us. Fix this, please.*

He told me that he didn't want to talk to me at that moment. Although it was hard to hang up the phone, I knew I had to. I never wanted to be the type of girlfriend that pushed a relationship. I wanted it to be a two-way street. Though it seemed I had been the one to mess it up, I didn't want to ruin it. So, I hung up the phone.

Much later that afternoon, I laid across my bed and thought of my new predicament. It was raining outside. Thunder and lightning were filling the dismal sky. Just as I couldn't stop the hail from hitting my windowpane, I couldn't stop Tad from wanting to pull away from me.

My dad entered, saying, "I'm really disappointed in you, Payton. Hanging with a guy that ain't about nothing—"

"You don't understand. You've got Tad figured wrong," I tried explaining.

"Payton, don't try lying to me. I saw what I saw. Now I'm serious. You better watch yourself, young lady. We won't always be able to watch out for you."

My dad left my room. The dark setting around me sunk me deeper into depression. I realized I had to get out of this gloomy state. There had to be some type of way to resolve this. And although it hadn't come to me yet, I hoped a good night's rest could surely fix this.

That Monday morning I was at my locker. Although I didn't want to be at school, I proceeded to get my books for first period. Lynzi walked up to me full of the energy I lacked.

"Girl, I'd been calling you and calling you all day yesterday. Your phone just rang. Where were you?" She attacked as if I owed her an explanation. "And your machine didn't come on either."

"Well hon', thanks to you, I don't have a phone. My parents took it, okay?" I told her as I slammed my locker door shut.

"Girl, you know I wasn't in my right frame of mind," Lynzi pestered as she followed me to my class.

"Well it seems like you should have thought of that before now. Taken one less drink, maybe? Especially when you're going over to another's house. Then maybe you wouldn't have destroyed stuff and not remembered. You know what, Lynzi? I don't even know why I waste my time. The look you just gave, like 'What did I do?' Shhh—I don't even have time." I threw my hand in her face and walked away.

After a long day at school, I finally made it to my Jeep. Since I didn't have a phone and Tad refused to talk to me on one anyway, I figured I'd swing by his school. Silver Bluff wasn't too far. Though it was in South Carolina, it would only be a twenty-minute drive.

I hoped that if Tad saw me in person, he'd want to talk through our problems. *Surely,* I told myself, *he wouldn't turn me away.* Even if he gave me a hard time, I wasn't planning to come back to Georgia until he and I were cool.

Before I could open up the door, Dymond leaned up against it. It was extremely irritating because she had a smile from one side of her cheek to the other. I had seen nothing all day worth smiling about.

"You know our girls are mad at each other. I saw both of them at different times today and they each told me that you were mad at them," she said.

I was angry at her too. They must not have told her that part. Got some nerve being all up in my face like we were cool.

She continued, "We were just having fun and things got a little out of control. There's no need to carry a grudge with them. Why are you not saying anything? Oh, OK, you're supposed to be mad at me, too."

"By George, I think she's got it," I articulated with sarcasm.

"I ain't do nothin'," Dymond sternly protested, "for you to be mad at me!"

"How dare you say that to me. My mom showed me, this morning, where you took one of the wine bottles from the china cabinet and drank it."

"She had seven of them," Dymond said to me. "Shoot, it might've even been ten. I didn't think she'd miss one. Plus, it wasn't a big bottle; it was just a little somethin'. For real, for real, I mean, I didn't think she'd even miss it. How did you know it was us anyway?"

Huffing, I breathed, "Out of process of elimination, Dymond, that's how. Rain and Lynzi were in my parents' room, otherwise caught up in mess, causing trouble. So, I figured it had to be you. And just so you know, there were eight of those bottles. They came from my parents' wedding. They've had them for years, since before I was born. That's something you'll never be able to replace. They don't even make those little bottles anymore. You should have known it was special, knowing that my parents don't drink. They saved them from their wedding and intended to split half of them and drink some at my wedding and drink some at Perry's wedding. Now we're a bottle short, thanks to your greediness. I gotta go. It's like you guys care about no one but yourselves. All that's important is wanting to have a good time. You invited yourself over to my house—"

"Well, it wasn't like you refused," Dymond cut in.

"No, I didn't refuse, but you could tell it was uncomfortable for me. My boyfriend didn't even want to be around you guys. Now he doesn't even want to be around me!" I yelled.

I opened my car door with such force that it scooted Dymond over enough for me to get in. She pushed the door shut, flipped her hand in the air, and stormed away. I could care less if she had an attitude. Basically, they had ruined my doggone life, and I couldn't dismiss that, especially when they don't think that they've done wrong. All three of them irked my last nerve.

Good, his car is still here, I thought as I pulled in the back of Silver Bluff High School. Since we didn't have to cheer anymore, I got out early. Silver Bluff was still in school, and that was a good thing, since I'd driven all this way. The last thing I'd want was for Tad to have already left. I was determined he was going to talk to me. Whether he liked it or not, he was going to hear me out. Surely he still wanted our relationship. Deep in my heart, I felt that he still cared.

Sitting in the car waiting for him to come out was beginning to annoy me. It seemed as if everyone was coming out of school but Tad. After fifteen minutes, I decided I wasn't going to wait any longer. I stepped out of the Jeep and headed inside the school, even though I was not a student. Knowing good and well I should have checked in at the office, I didn't. I figured since I wasn't going to be there for that long, it wasn't a necessity. Just my luck, as I turned the corner, I ran into the principal.

"Young lady, what is your name? I don't think you're a student at this school," the older gentleman questioned.

"Uh, no sir, I'm not. It was just an—"

He enforced, "Don't try tripping over your words or

make up some excuse to tell me. You march right over there to the office and check in before you go walking around this school. With all the stuff going on nowadays, we have to account for every person in this building."

"Yes sir," I said to him.

As I turned around to head back towards the office, I went down another strange corridor. Tad was pent up at a locker with a girl I knew. It was Val Austin, another debutante, who'd had a crush on him forever. I didn't want to assume anything. That's why there was so much strife between Tad and me a few weeks ago. I'd assumed he was with Starr and he'd assumed I was with Dakari. All kinds of drama because no one wanted to communicate.

As I stepped closer, I was shocked by what my eyes saw. I didn't have to assume anything; they showed me more than I wanted to imagine. Seeing this chick leaning on Tad's shoulder and then placing a kiss on his cheek left me no alternative but to be furious.

"Excuse me, but why are you kissin' my boyfriend?" I stunned them both as I opened my mouth.

Stepping away from the girl and closer to me, Tad asked, "What are you doing here, Payton?"

His tone wasn't a pleasant one, and the compassion I had for him was gone. Two angry people faced with whether or not to continue a relationship. It didn't seem like we were about to continue.

"I thought I was coming to see my boyfriend, *my* boyfriend. Yet, I find you accepting kisses from somebody else. That's not assuming anything; that's what I witnessed. She almost kissed you on the lips! What's going on?" I bullied.

"Tad babe, I'll talk to you later. We can continue what we started then," the girl said, trying to rattle my cage.

She was successful at doing that. I was a wreck inside. We weren't even officially broken up and yet he had something to finish with someone else, some other girl, some girl he knows really likes him. And not trying to be funny, but she's got nothing on me.

"You know I told you I wasn't ready to talk to you right now. I was thinking through some things," Tad said.

"How can you think through some things," I lashed out, "if you're being entertained and distracted by others?"

"Well, I hate to walk away and leave you all high-strung. But I really need to think, and you're not making it easy. I'll be in touch. I gotta go, but just so you know, there's nothing going on with me and that girl. You are my girlfriend. And until we both know that's different, you won't ever have to worry about me being with someone else. What you saw isn't what's going on. I helped her with a school project and she just thanked me. I'd never cheat on you," Tad earnestly explained.

He left. Left me in a hallway that was unfamiliar to me, just like the feelings I was getting from him were so unfamiliar. I was losing my privileges at home. I was losing my friends because they didn't care about me. Now, it seemed I was losing my guy. And if not to someone else, it still hurt that I might lose him, period.

Maybe I brought all of this on myself? No, no I did bring all this on myself. Trying to be grown, I wanted to celebrate in a way that wasn't pleasing to God. I guess I didn't want to own up to that fact, but now I had to, and oh how it hurt as I was left suffering the consequences.

Traveling to Love

"M om, where are we going?" I questioned as we drove out of Georgia and into South Carolina.

"Just sit tight; we'll be there in a second," she looked over briefly and told me, without really telling me anything.

A week had come and gone. This was the beginning of spring break. My friends and I had been planning for so long to go to Myrtle Beach together. Needless to say, with all the drama they had recently caused me, the trip was off.

This Saturday was supposed to be a time for me to sit, relax, and find myself. Figure out what I wanted from me. Tad hadn't thought it necessary to call me, and I realized I couldn't let my life revolve around him. Earlier in the school year, I had made that same mistake in chasing Dakari. I refused to sink to that level anymore. I was going to swim, and if I had to swim by myself, then that's what it was going to be. I had Christ, and as long as He understood me, my life was going to be better than OK.

Mom and I pulled up to a restaurant in South Carolina.

There were a few cars there that looked a little familiar. There was a white Cadillac, and when I looked at the license plate, it confirmed it was Rain's mom's car. Then I saw a cute black BMW that we all loved. I was certain it belonged to Lynzi's mom. I was certain because next to it was a beat-up yellow clunker that Dymond's mom drove everywhere.

"Mom, what's going on?" I asked as we parked.

"Don't worry about it."

We walked to a table set for eight. My former friends were sitting beside their mothers. My mom and I sat in the empty seats. There were lots of frowns on lots of faces. I'm sure my mother cooked up the whole thing, but what the purpose was I had no idea. We had traveled thirty-five minutes to come to this restaurant, which I had never been to, and although the atmosphere was warm, my immediate table was sending chills.

My mother began talking about how disappointed she was in all four of us young ladies. None of us probably wanted to hear this lecture, but we listened intently anyway. I was also a little embarrassed that my mom had told everyone's mother what took place. It was bad enough that I had to get in trouble. Even though I was mad at my friends, I didn't want them to get punished.

"Now you ladies are about to graduate," my mom preached. "We're about to trust you guys to step out into this crazy world and live on your own. There's tons of stuff going on nowadays. I would just like to think that you can take care of yourself and not make stupid choices. Alcohol is no joke. It is for people to drink when they're a certain age. When you're twenty-one, you're at least a little bit more mature. Now, I'm not advocating drinking at all, but you ladies don't even meet the legal age requirement. I just think we need to have a talk about that because we care about you all a great deal."

Dymond's mother voiced, "And Dymond, you know better. We have too many drunk folks in our family that can't even pay their bills 'cause they're going to the package store trying to buy a six-pack of this or a shot of that. You know the effects. You should be smarter, girl, way smarter."

"And Rain, you know we had a cousin that died from driving while under the influence. I wouldn't have thought you'd have touched the stuff either." Rain's mom looked at her with compassion and said, "I'm trying to understand, baby, but Keith died."

Then Lynzi's mom said, "The reason why I let you taste stuff at *home*, Lynzi, is because you're so hot-to-trot to want to taste some. My only requirement was that you never do it outside the house because it could be dangerous. Now why would you go over to somebody else's house and drink? Just consider that privilege revoked."

We all felt pretty bad. And that common bond made us come together and realize that we did need to hold each other accountable to the good things. We all apologized for our behavior and enjoyed the lunch with our moms. It had been the one and only time all eight of us had been together, and how I wished we'd done that a lot sooner. They never had to apologize to me for all the craziness that went on a week ago, but being at that table, being united as one made us forgive and forget and look forward to the good stuff ahead.

Lynzi had always been my friend, but she cared about herself more than anyone else. So I was surprised when she stepped out and said, "I guess I owe everybody an apology. My friends, my mom, you guys' moms . . . I just . . . well . . . it was my boyfriend who brought all that stuff to the Civic Center. He kinda encouraged everybody to try it and then he . . . um . . . he just kinda invited himself over to Payton's house. I could've told him no, but I wanted to enjoy the night, and I guess I started a lot of the trouble."

"Wait, wait, wait a minute. Your escort had the alcohol?

I thought it was Tad," my mom voiced in disbelief.

"Tad? Ha!" Dymond laughed.

Rain cut in and said, "Tad Taylor? Noooo, he wasn't even drinkin'!"

Lynzi cut in and voiced, "He was the one who tried to tell us not to. To be honest, I thought he was being a nerd, but had we listened, then maybe we wouldn't be in this position."

My mom looked at me and placed her hand on my shoulder. She then sweetly caressed my hand. I felt the remorse she must have been feeling for her and my father to wrongfully accuse my guy. They never even wanted to hear an explanation for why Tad was holding all those cans. Since Tad wasn't trying to talk to me, and my parents were so mad, I hadn't even forced the issue in the last couple of days, but now it had all come out.

Looking honestly in her eyes, I explained with her full attention, "It was pretty unfortunate, the timing that you and Dad came home. Tad was trying to help me so I wouldn't get in trouble. He picked up some of the cans that were laying around the house. I know it sounds bad for cans to even be picked up, but Rain was right; Tad had never drunk any of them. He's a great guy," I politicized, as if I was his campaign manager.

"Can ya'll believe we're going to Myrtle Beach?" Lynzi exclaimed her happiness.

All four of us were packed in my Jeep. Seniors, friends, spring breakers. We were headed a little short of three hours away, and I couldn't believe we were making the journey.

A couple of other schools from Augusta were out at the same time. Even some from the surrounding areas like Aiken, South Carolina, where Tad's school is located, were out as well. The word had spread that this year's senior class would be partying in Myrtle Beach, and we looked forward to having a blast.

I had truly learned my lesson about dabbling and dipping in things that I'm not supposed to. I wondered if Rain, Lynzi, and Dymond had learned their lesson as well. The temptation that we had faced just a week ago would be out on the lure once again. These beaches were going to be full of underaged kids drinking some of everything, and I just couldn't seem to think that my friends wouldn't want a taste.

So as I drove and we played our music, all movin' and groovin' to the beat, I turned down the sound and said, "So what's up ya'll? No drinkin', right?"

"Of course not," Rain quickly responded.

Dymond and Lynzi were in the back. They looked at each other and let out a giggle. I was watching them in the rearview mirror. The sight disturbed me. Though they didn't say it, I knew they were making no promises not to drink.

"Ya'll, I don't want it around me. I'm telling you now. I've gotten into too much trouble with you guys, and I am not going back down that road again. Ya'll can get out of the car, do whatever you want to do. Ya'll can sit someplace else—"

"Calm down, calm down, calm down!" Dymond said from the back of the car. "Girl, you know we lookin' out for you. You know we ain't gon' mess up. Daaang! This is supposed to be a good time. Ain't nobody supposed to be all heated and upset. Just chill out and enjoy. We cool."

"What's that saying? If you do me wrong once, shame on you. If you do me wrong twice, shame on me. Well, you guys won't be getting me twice," I breathed, seriously upset.

Rain tried to keep a cool head. She reached over and turned up the music. I could see her smiling face, but I saw nothing funny or nothing to smile about.

The first night of our stay in Myrtle Beach had been rather interesting. Though we didn't see anyone from home, we met some really crazy, cool kids. Braxton, Alec, and Trey were the three guys staying in the condo next to us. As soon as we pulled up to our door, these gents were hovering around us, trying to help us unpack. Naturally, Lynzi thought it was too cute. I, on the other hand, was apprehensive. I mean, although it was spring break and they looked our age, I didn't know them and wasn't too excited about getting to know them.

Now don't misunderstand me. They were some cuties, very nice on the eyes. However, two of them came off too strong. Braxton sensed I wasn't that comfortable with them and he approached me a different way. He was nice and kind, not cocky like the other two. Over the course of the evening we became buddies.

"So, uh, got a boyfriend, pretty lady?" I remember him saying to me as we talked outside the condo later that first night.

"Actually, I don't even know how to respond to that," I told him with the utmost sincerity.

Did my heart still belong to Tad? Although I wanted it to, maybe that fact alone wasn't enough to keep me being his girl. Braxton explained that he didn't want anything from me. Just a guy about to graduate and wanting to have some fun before that happened. He told me his only agenda was making new friends. Before I realized, the ten minutes I had intended to speak to him turned into an hour.

I ended spilling my guts, probably because my parents couldn't understand where I was coming from, and my friends were so into themselves that they didn't want to hear it either. And the guy I wished I could talk to at this time didn't want to talk to me. Luckily, there was another gentleman who cared enough to listen.

And after hearing it all, he softly said, "Well, this guy will be a fool to break up with you because of that. And true enough, I drink. I'm not as wise as the brother you're speaking about, although I do know I should abstain from the stuff. He shouldn't hold you accountable or punish you because you wanted to try it. But, maybe you learned your lesson."

With energy, I said, "I have, oh really I have. Toasting at my deb ball was really anticlimactic."

He continued, "Well, that's what you need to tell this guy of yours. You need to make him see that he was right. You need to let him know that he means more to you than trouble."

He seemed to be giving such wise counsel. It was as if he was sent straight to me to tell me all of this. Then we got to my condo. It was as if we had stepped out of our quiet zone and into the crazy house. Both his friends and mine were having a blast. What I liked about it was that it was as if they were on a natural high. No drugs, no alcohol, and no cigarettes to aid in the fun. So it was easy for Braxton and I to join in and enjoy the moment. We were a bunch of kids happier than little ones at Christmas, opening the toys they'd wanted all year.

The next night we found our friends. Myrtle Beach wasn't a big place, but since it was last-minute that the four of us were definitely going, we never really got in touch with our crew to see where they were staying. I didn't even know if Tad was coming up there. Rain paged Tyson, so before we woke up the next morning, he was standing in all of our faces. Apparently, Rain had left a key under the mat for him. We didn't like Rain leaving the key like that. What if people went around checking mats? After all, this is spring break; anything could happen. So taking every safety precaution is a must. Plus, Lynzi had rollers all in her hair and a frou frou nightgown that was surely not something a guy would want to see.

Lynzi woke up in a panic when she saw Tyson standing before us. "Oh my gosh, oh my gosh!" she yelled hysterically as she rushed to the bathroom. "I don't want you to see me like this. Oh my gosh!"

"Tyson, what are you doing here?" I said to him groggily.

After he explained to me his position and Rain came to his defense, I still let him know how much I didn't appreciate him coming in without knocking.

"Well, look Pay, I paid rent here just like you guys. I don't have to get your permission. I wanted him to be here. We're going to do some things together. So he's here. I was planning to be ready, but I overslept a little bit. It's no big deal. Plus, I don't know what Lynzi's trippin' about. It's not like my man was lookin' at her anyway."

Dymond pulled up the covers on her large body and uttered, "Well girl, he didn't have to come in our bedroom and stuff. Daaang."

"Oh, I'm sorry, ladies. I'm sorry," Tyson said as he backed out the door.

Rain got up and went to the bathroom. I tried to lie back down and go to sleep, but my slumber was interrupted as I heard commotion going on in the bathroom. It seemed as if Lynzi and Rain were going at it again. Which only naturally made sense because they never really resolved the "Tyson issue." Lynzi's comment about not wanting Tyson to see her looking bad made for problems.

"Girl, hold up, hold up! See? I knew you wanted my man. If you didn't, why would you care what you looked like? Why would you care?" I heard Rain yell.

"It's the principle of the thing," Lynzi argued. "Don't trip! It's the principle of the thing. I don't want no guy seeing me like this. I got a man, OK? I got a man."

Rain retorted, "Huh, you think you got one. Yeah right, you know you can't get in touch with Bam now. He's probably talking to some girls from who-knows-where. You just don't want to be alone, so you try to steal my guy."

"Steal him?!" Lynzi looked at her and said. "If I wanted the brother, I could get him. Believe dat!"

As Rain swung her hand to hit Lynzi, Dymond and I busted into the bathroom and broke the tension. I couldn't believe it had come to this. This was nonsense.

I let out in frustration, "We all just need a break. Everybody just needs to go their own way. OK?"

"We came up here for fun, ya'll. Stop trippin'," Dymond told them.

Tyson didn't even know what was going on. He was out in the car waiting for Rain to come out. I didn't even realize thirty minutes had passed. I guess I had fallen asleep some.

After Rain stormed out of the house, Lynzi looked at Dymond and me and verbalized, "I need to go shopping. I need to spend some money. I'm too mad. Too angry. I can't believe this chick thinks that she is all that and can talk to me any way. I better go spend some money 'fore I go off on somebody else."

Much later that evening, the three of us got ready to go out. We hadn't run into Rain all day, and because of what happened earlier this morning, that was a good thing. Dymond thought she knew the name of the hotel where Fatz and Bam were staying. Although I wasn't trying to see their men, I didn't have any other plans. So I agreed to tag along to help them find their beaus.

There were people everywhere. More specifically, black folks were everywhere. It was cool. After searching about three different places that Dymond thought her friends might be, we stumbled up and saw some other folks from our school at the Holiday Inn South. Bam and Fatz couldn't be too far away, and if they weren't at that place, I had planned to head back to the condo. Dymond and Lynzi could look for them themselves, I thought. I was tired of searching for someone else's guy.

Maybe that was a wrong feeling, but as it got harder and harder to find them, I wondered if they wanted to be found. As the music I loved so much played at the place, the three of us stepped onto the dance floor and started jammin'.

"Hey, ho, hey, ho, hey, ho!" the crowd chanted together, arms waving in the air.

The latest dance brought us all to the dance floor. Everyone kinda shuffled together, scooted to one side, then scooted to another side, stepped back a few steps, and then stepped up a few steps. It was cool. The dance started at our high school earlier in the year. I guess it was kinda like our senior dance, and there we were doing it in Myrtle Beach.

I turned to Lynzi and said, "Girl, I think Bam just went around the corner. Yeah, that's him over there."

She left the dance floor, and I continued to get down. Had I known what was about to happen, I wouldn't have ever told her who I saw. When the dance was over and she didn't come back, Dymond and I went to find her. What we found was Bam, arm-in-arm with a preppie looking blond. It took everything I had to hold back my anger. Lynzi stood before us in tears, and Dymond spoke for us all.

"You give a joker like you a chance and you trip! You trip! Trying to get everybody here! I bet you're just in dog heaven," she lashed.

"Lynzi, you know me, girl," he tried to explain. "I gotta get my groove on. I can't be tied down. I ain't gon' do right. You better off without me. Plus Yancy and I, we got thangs to discuss."

Bam selfishly turned to this girl he called "Yancy," and kissed her! Lynzi was too numb to do anything. I grabbed her hand and pulled her away. She didn't need to see that. And she certainly didn't deserve to be hurt so intensely. Although I didn't want to, at that moment I detested Bam. The hard look in Lynzi's eyes told me I wasn't the only one who felt that way.

"He ain't even worth it, girl. He ain't even worth it," I tried to coax my friend into believing.

Dymond stayed at the Holiday Inn South. She found Fatz and he agreed to bring her back to the condo. The ride back with Lynzi wasn't fun. Looking over at my friend, she appeared so dejected. My heart was tearing into shreds as I saw every tear stream from her face. It reminded me of October when we were both in the car talking about our male problems. I had just found out Dakari didn't want to be with me, and she found out Bam had cheated on her with Starr's cousin.

We were there for each other then. When it was hard, we were always there for each other. Although I didn't want to admit it, I still had man problems. And it was obvious she did too. That was hard. The drive seemed endless.

Although no words were exchanged, I was where she was. Two souls connected by dejection. We desperately wanted something we couldn't have. Neither of us knew if we'd reach our goal or if we should just give up. For me, some decision had to be made soon. I was tired of never fully reaching happiness in a relationship. It seemed I was always traveling to love.

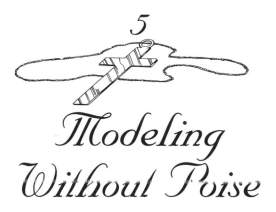

Modeling Without Poise

"Why is this happening to me?" Lynzi let out in despair as we drove back to our Myrtle Beach condo. "Why does every relationship I have not work out?"

"What are you talking about? Bam has been your only boyfriend."

"Yeah, but we've been off and on for years. My parents, they aren't even together. I don't know. Maybe I'm just such a mean, horrible person that I deserve it—to be alone and miserable," she ranted.

"You don't mean that," I tried convincing her.

"Ohhhh yes I do. Look at what I said to Rain, telling her I could have her guy. Everybody knows Tyson would never leave her, and plus I don't want him. I just didn't want anyone to see me lookin' all crazy. I never thought she'd take it the wrong way," Lynzi sighed in despair. "I don't know what I'm gonna do with this Bam situation. I love him and it's obvious he doesn't care about me or what I think. I don't know how I'm gonna get over him."

Finally we reached the place we were calling home. As soon as we got inside we heard a car pull up. It pulled up rather harshly, so we both assumed it was Bam trying to come back and take back his mistake. We weren't having it, both she and I agreed. She did not need to talk to this chump. However, knowing Lynzi like I did, if she went out there and dealt with him, she'd give in to his "I'm sorry."

"You stay here, girl. I'll handle this. I'll tell him you do not want to see him. You stay here," I asserted, making sure Lynzi didn't move a muscle.

As I opened the door to go off on Bam, my eyes were delighted when they laid upon Tad Taylor. *Wow,* I thought! *Wow!* It was as if he were a superstar. I was just that honored and happy to see him.

"What are you doing here?" I softly spoke, "I assumed since I hadn't run into you, you had changed your vacation destination. And now you're standing here before me. Have you been in town for a while?"

He stepped up to the door and kissed me softly on the cheek. Although just a peck, it sure was meaningful. Then he held me tight.

"I care for you so much, Payton. First, I thought you should be where I am in my walk with Christ. Then I realized that it takes a lot of things to grow in Him, and that I can't expect you to be there overnight, but I want you to get there. I want you to love Christ with all your heart and soul. Maybe I can help you find what I have, but I can't do that if I am a jerk and not with you."

I questioned, "How'd you find me? I never told you where I was staying."

"I went to your parents' house. Actually, I forgot you were going out of town. With the punishment you were on, I just assumed you weren't going. They apologized to me for accusing me of all that alcohol junk and gave me the number to where I could find you. I've been calling all day and there was no answer. So I took the directions down from the person who rents the condos and got in my car and drove up here."

Elated and surprised, I replied, "You mean you been on the road all night just to see me?"

"Yeah, the drive didn't bother me. You were on my mind all the way. So with a good thought to think about, it was no problem at all," Tad responded like a character from a romance novel.

"Tell him I'll talk to him," Lynzi let out in desperation as she opened the condo door.

She was extremely disappointed when she saw it was Tad. I felt her anguish. Lynzi grabbed my keys from the nightstand with one hand and her purse with the other. Slinging the black and lavender bag across her shoulder, she practically hit me in the face.

"I—I—I gotta go. I—I—I gotta drive your car. I—I'll be back," she said as she rushed over to my car.

"Be back in a sec," I kindly said to Tad.

I followed her out to my car. Though I felt her despair, I was still rational. My good friend, however, was acting crazy.

I pleaded, "You're in no position to drive. You're all upset. Come back in."

"Just please don't bother me, Pay. Just please . . . just please let me go. Let me do this. Please! I just . . . I just . . . I just need to think. Don't worry about me. Enjoy your guy. At least only one of us is alone now, instead of two. I'll be back before you know it. I . . . I really am OK," Lynzi explained, sounding sane.

I stepped back from the car. Lynzi's eyes told me thanks. I only hoped I wouldn't regret my decision to let her drive alone.

"It's good to see you. I really, really miss being with you. I realized that there are some things I need to tell you. I'm sorry. I was wrong. You made my night special, but I chose my friends over you," I told Tad inside awhile later that night.

"I wasn't angry 'cause you put your friends before me," he softly spoke, looking into my eyes as he held my hand gently. "I was really frustrated because you put everything before God."

I couldn't respond. He was right. Going back to the night when I first let alcohol touch my lips and filter my mind, not only did I owe Tad an apology, but more importantly, I owed God one. I couldn't just apologize to say it. I had to have a mission, a purpose, a goal for keeping me on the path that was pleasing to God daily. I had to make sure I didn't fall into temptation.

My peers couldn't give a firm foundation. And though my boyfriend was a strong believer, I knew that it was my responsibility to live godly.

We had been friends for years; I didn't want to put my girlfriends down. So I set out in my mind to change them. Make them want to be like me, and live a life for Christ.

Rain and Tyson busted through the door laughing. She grabbed my arm and pulled me into the bathroom.

"I want to be with Tyson. I want to be with a man who cares. I think I'm gonna do it!" Rain pronounced with pride.

"I know you think you like him and all, but that's crazy. Actually, that's the most ridiculous thing I've ever heard. How dare you even think about giving yourself to this guy? Be smart. Don't be stupid."

"I wasn't thinking about being with him that way; it's a sin."

"You better quit trippin' and think with a clear head. Don't be so hot; it's totally not attractive anyway."

"Don't preach to me." Rain stormed off in front of me in tears.

"C'mon, Tyson, let's go,"

As I came out of the bedroom Tad said to me, "You were a little harsh on your friend, huh?"

"Wait. Wait. Hold on." I kinda brushed him off and uttered, "I need to talk to that chick."

Tyson's car sped out of the parking lot. Just as I was about to go back in, I noticed Fatz's funky white minivan parked nearby. It had only a flicker of light on inside the light-tinted window. To irk me further, the music was blasting. The beat was thumping so much that the car was jumping.

"It looks like everybody wanted to get a little frisky tonight," I mumbled to myself.

I had a strange feeling what Dymond and Fatz were engaged in, and it enraged me. I opened one door and was very shocked at what I found. Dymond had a little white piece of paper in her mouth; small puffs filled the air.

"Heeyyy girl," she said, clearly out of it. "C'mon in, Pay. C'mon in."

I screamed, "Are you absolutely crazy! Girl, you could go to jail! If you don't get out of the car right now—"

"You're not my mother," Dymond lashed out.

"Hmph, I know, but I'll call her. Get out now!"

Dymond finally got out and Tad helped me help her into our safe haven. Although I was disappointed in Fatz, I couldn't let him leave either. I know we all thought we were grown, but this was a little much. And although I do understand wanting to try things, some things you just can't try. Too dangerous. Too risky. Too fatal. It's too against God's will.

Dymond yelled, "We just saw Lynzi. You gon' save her, too . . . Miss High-And-Mighty? She 'bout to enter a wet T-shirt contest."

After taking the keys from Fatz to secure their safety, Tad and I headed to rescue my other friend. We got there just in time; she was about to go up. Her T-shirt was soaked and sticking to her body, and although her figure was cute, there was no reason she needed to be parading it. The jeans she left the house in were now cut to short shorts, up in places they didn't need to be.

When I ran over to her before she stepped onto the stage, looking strangely provocative, she opened her mouth and breathed, "Get away from me. Got thangs to take care of. I don't need a sitter." Her breath reeked of liquor as she ranted.

I don't know when she drank or where she got it, but her red eyes also told me she was not in her right mind. As I reached to grab her again, she pushed me back.

"I said get out of the way!"

I fell down two steps, not hard, but enough to get the point that she didn't want to come down. Tad came to my side and said, "I've seen the way you've been talking to all three of your friends tonight, and I gotta tell you, you're not reaching them."

"Tad I—I want them—I want them to think like me. I want them to please God and—and—look at them. All of them have lost their minds. One is gettin' high, one is gettin' drunk, and the other is trying to get with her guy. I wanted to be an example. I wanted them to be like me."

"Well you can't dictate to them how they need to lead their lives. Show them. Show them through how you live yours. Reel them in. Don't push them away."

Just then, I watched my girlfriend walk across the stage, showing off her physical form to tons of screaming jerks. As she could hardly stand, I knew I needed to get through to her. Tad was right. Maybe I, too, was modeling without poise.

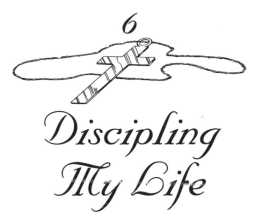

6

Discipling My Life

"W ell, that's interesting," Billie said to me as she started taking off my fingernail polish. "Hearing about what's going on with your friends is interesting, but I'm sure you have something going on that you need to talk about. Something Payton is struggling with, not everybody else's struggle. So what's really going on with you and this new boyfriend of yours? Tell me your business."

I guess I was kind of gossiping. I never really thought about it. She was always so easy to talk to. I could just sit there and let her do my nails, let her do my toes, and out comes everything. I had no intention of saying a word before I sat down, but she makes me so relaxed. She is such a good role model. Although she does my nails, I totally look up to her. Not to say that a nail buffer isn't important, but it wasn't like she was a doctor or anything.

Yet this Christian woman always got me thinking, and this time I didn't know if I was really ready to think about me. I didn't really know what was going on. Yeah, there were some issues, probably a ton of them, but I wasn't really sure where to start.

"I don't know. That's tough," I huffed and replied.

"Tough? Explain," she said. "Tell me more. Tell me more."

"I told you about the drama all my friends are going through, and if you ask me, their lives are a mess. I wanna help them when I see them going down the path of destruction, but they won't let me. I want to stop them from the fall I see in front of them. They all need help. I don't understand. Now, I'm not saying I have all the answers, but the answers I do have would help. I mean, if we were taking a test, they would probably look on my paper to cheat. So why can't they let me help them out here when my advice or answer is totally legit?"

"Sometimes people have to find out the hard way."

"Well, they are about to find out the hard way," I said, shaking my head as she gently took the polish off my last nail. "I mean, if they don't listen to me, they're going to get in serious trouble, and that's really a problem for me because I just believe they don't respect me enough. They all think I don't know what I'm talking about, and I do. I do!"

"So why are you defending your position so heavily? I sense tension. I sense anxiety. I sense that maybe you really aren't sure—that you're questioning things yourself. Do you have it all together? Do you have their answers?"

As she started working on my cuticles, I started pondering her question. I didn't think I was unsure, but maybe I was. I knew the answer was God, Jesus, and the Holy Spirit, along with the Bible, but I couldn't quote more than three or four verses to back me up.

"OK, OK, I have some issues. I'm not sure where I need to be in my walk with Christ, and that kinda bothers me. Especially when my boyfriend, who knows way more than me, doesn't know everything either."

"No, he doesn't know everything," she gently cut in and

said. "We won't know everything 'til we're with Him. We all fall short of the glory of God. You should be hard on yourself when it comes to your growth as a Christian, but you shouldn't be so hard on yourself that you don't want to get better. I gotta be honest with you, Payton—people don't want to follow you if they know your flaws. Your obvious ones. You've got to get yourself together. You must understand what it is to have Him in you. You gotta be able to live that, and people have to see you and know it. And until you're there, until you're happy with it, until you have peace, until you're walking by faith, no one will believe what you say. 'Cause you yourself aren't even sure."

It hurt me that my friends were hurting. It bothered me that they had concerns. It worried me to no end, but she was right. I had to get a grip on me, and then I'd be able to help them. Being so intimidated with Tad's knowledge of Christ wasn't helping me either. I gotta know His words. I gotta stand up for what I believe. It all sounded good, but how would I do it?

I left the shop with pretty nails, pretty toes, a cute hairdo, and a head full of confusion. I was excited, yet bewildered, but I was determined to find the answers. This seasoned lady of grace told me I could call her some time and she would disciple me. I was too embarrassed to tell her that I didn't know what discipling meant. Hopefully, that too would change.

"Mama! Doorbell!" I yelled through the house.

"Get it, honey! I'm in the kitchen."

"Get the door, Perry," I tried convincing my brother.

"I'm in the bathroom. You get it."

"Great. Just great," I let out with frustration. "Just as I start studying the Bible, I get an interruption."

I had been studying my Bible, reading in John, learning

about Jesus' life on the earth. My rationale was that that was as good a place as any for me to start to learn how to have a closer walk with Jesus. All the way to the door, I had no clue why my mom couldn't take a break and open it. Surely it was one of the neighbors, or some salesman or somebody that most assuredly wasn't for me. To my surprise, I opened the door and it was Tad.

"What are you doing here?" I said to him with a huge smile on my face.

"Your parents invited me over for dinner. I didn't know it was a surprise to you, but I hope you're happy to have me."

"Of course I'm happy to have you. I just wish my mom would have told me. Actually, in her own unique way, she did tell me. She told me to get cute for dinner, and I thought she was having company. Someone not important to me. So I kinda blew it off. Next time I'll listen to Mom!" I told him in a joking way as I ushered him to the living room.

Before he sat down in the chair, he reached his arms out to me and gave me a hug.

"How've you been?" he asked in concern.

"OK. I don't know. I'm stressed. I can't lie to you," I told him with sincerity. "I'm just kinda confused about a lot of stuff, and I'm trying to get it together. Here, let me take this."

He handed me a bottle of Welch's Sparkling Grape Juice, with the cutest little bow around it. I grabbed Tad's hand and led him into the kitchen where my mom was. When I handed her the bottle, she smiled.

"Thank you for inviting me to dinner," my gentleman friend said.

"This is so sweet of you. You didn't have to do this, but we thank you. We'll have it for dinner."

"Sorry we misjudged you," my dad said to Tad, as we sat down at the dining room table.

When I looked over at Tad's face I could tell he was struggling with something, like he wanted to say something but couldn't. My parents sensed his anxiety as well. They gave a look back that made Tad feel comfortable to say whatever was on his mind. My guy did just that.

He shocked us all when he said these words: "No sir, you don't owe me an apology. I think I'm the one that really owes you guys one. Sure, I wasn't drinking and I'm all free and clear of being accused of that. I owe you an apology because I never got your permission to be over at your house when you weren't here. I think the agreement was I would see your daughter to the door like a gentleman and go my merry way. That's not what happened. See, I went along to get along, and it really got me in trouble. Trouble that I deserved. So in essence, what you accused me of, I got myself into because I shouldn't have been someplace that you didn't expect to see me."

I think even my younger brother Perry was blown away by Tad's mature comment. I never even thought of that. I never really gave much thought that my parents never said it was OK for me to have guests over. Tad was right. When my friends asked or invited themselves over, I had no right to accept or even say it was OK. This is my house, but at this time, I don't make the rules. Next year in college, I will be making some rules, but right now is not next year and Tad was the only one who recognized that.

My father was sitting beside Tad. He leaned over and patted him on the back. That was his way of saying he more than approved of the statement Tad just made. My mom smiled and said, "Since we were all wrong in some sense or another, let's just store it all away so we won't make the same mistakes." My mom said. "All is forgiven. Sound good?"

"It's great with me," my little brother Perry said as he dug into his food.

"Boy, get your hands back. Ain't nobody said no prayers

around here," my dad voiced as he popped Perry's hand.

We all bowed our heads and my father began, "Heavenly Father, I thank You for this opportunity to be gathered at this table with my family. Lord, we take too much for granted sometimes, and as I look around at my wife and my two children, I realize how blessed a man I really am. I thank You, Father, for my daughter's friend, Lord, who loves You and is a great influence on her. I pray, Lord, that these two will enjoy graduation and all the festivities in a way, Lord, that's pleasing and honoring to You. I thank You again for this meal we're about to receive. May it go to the nourishment of our bodies and our bodies to Your service. Amen."

For the next hour or so, our dinner conversation ranged from a wide selection of topics. We talked about Georgia football. My dad wanted to find out about Tad's training to see when he had to go to the University of Georgia in the summer for practice. My brother Perry was extremely interested, but Mom and I were clearly bored, so she moved the conversation to the prom.

Being that Tad and I went to two different schools, we had two different proms to attend. We had to decide which one we would attend, or if we would attend both. I naturally assumed we'd go to both. How could someone not want to go to their own prom? I didn't think there was any question that we wouldn't go to both, but when we started discussing it, I realized Tad couldn't care less. That bummed me out.

The dinner table with my parents, however, wasn't a place to discuss the matter with him. So I didn't say a word. Tad had to be convinced we'd go to both.

Perry interrupted the prom discussion when he brought up cheerleading tryouts at our high school. He wanted his little girlfriend to make it and asked if I could help her. I assured him I'd do everything I could, but I didn't want to give her too much of an advantage. When he got a little upset about that, my mom and dad teased him about having some serious feelings for this girl. He tried denying it, but then we asked him why he would care if she made it or not if he didn't really care about her. Perry was getting antsy and defensive. The more he seemed bothered, the more my daddy kept picking away.

Finally Tad broke in and said, "Hey man, there's nothing wrong with liking a young lady. Nothing wrong with showing her how much you care. Nothing wrong with letting other people know that you're not so tough after all."

I smiled from ear to ear.

After dinner, Tad and I walked the neighborhood. As I looked to the sky, I couldn't help but thank God for giving me such a great friend in the guy that stood beside me. Tad was definitely a gift I didn't deserve and did not want to lose. But in order to have a relationship with him, I couldn't think that I was unworthy. I couldn't be afraid of losing him and drive myself crazy. Out of that insecurity always comes problems. I just had to figure a way to be happy with me. To be happy with Payton. And then I could give him all he needed in a girlfriend. Someone with whom he could always be content and be proud to call "The girl who has my heart."

Interrupting my deep thoughts he asked, "What are you pondering over? I sense you're thinking about something over there."

"Yeah, I'm thinking about something good. I'm thinking about you."

I wasn't supposed to go there. I had made up my mind that I wasn't going there, but I went there anyway.

Looking into his eyes I said, "What in the world did I do to deserve such a guy? I'm crazy about you. You know that,

Tad Taylor? I'm crazy about you."

The wind was slightly blowing and it shifted some of my hair to my face. The gentleman before me brushed it back. Caressing my face, he made me feel very special.

"I say, Miss Payton Skky, we're both lucky. I'm very glad you're my lady. Ha ha ha ha—I bet you can't catch me!" he said as he tagged me and ran.

The two of us had so much fun together. It seemed like things were getting back on track with us. I knew there were deeper issues that we soon would have to face, like me being on the same level that he was on spiritually. Although we weren't there yet, I was determined to get there, and this time not for my guy's sake but for my God's.

To his amazement, I caught him. I won the race. It had been so long since I sprinted. It felt good though.

Before going in the house I breathed, "It's not you—I'm just good at track. I used to compete for the school, but I got tired and stopped."

"From how bad I just got beat," Tad said, "you better start back."

My parents liked Tad so much, the next day they allowed me to go to church with him. Since I don't get to see him Monday through Friday, I really appreciated making the most of our weekend. We were on our way to a restaurant, and I couldn't stop staring at Tad. The last time I'd seen him dressed up was the night of the Debutante Ball, and even though this wasn't a tuxedo, that blue pin-striped suit was looking mighty good on the brother.

"So, uh, where are we going? Now, we're having dinner with who?" I quizzed.

"Remember, last night I was telling you about the special teams' coach at my school. We're going to have dinner with him and his wife. He disciples me, and of course we've

64

been talking about you in our time together for a while now, and I thought it'd be neat if you two got to meet."

There was that word again. Disciple. Gosh, I had so many questions, but I didn't want to seem dumb, but here I was about to meet these people and I needed to educate myself, and since Tad knew more than me, I fired away with questions.

"What does that really mean? I mean, who disciples that man? Why do you even need someone to disciple you? I mean, you go to church. I don't understand."

"Well, discipling is a one-on-one relationship where there's someone who's a spiritual mentor of yours. I've been told it's better if they are older. That person gets into your life and cares about you, sometimes even instantly and grows you up in the Word. He helps you live by God's commandments," Tad explained.

"Oh . . . so it's much like the relationship Jesus had with the twelve disciples?" I quizzed.

He answered, "Yeah."

I was really interested. He saw my interest and smiled. Then he kept telling me all he knew.

"I've always been taught that in order to be a growing Christian you need to have someone disciple you. You need to have someone that's actually on the same level as you spiritually so that you encourage one another. That's called an accountability partner. Then you need to be discipling someone else so that you continue to use what you have to grow someone else up. Unfortunately, right now I only have one of the three. That's it. Someone that's discipling me. I think you'll really like Darius and Shayna. They are really sweet. Coach Mullen. He's cool. He's real cool."

Shayna Mullen was an absolutely adorable, short, petite lady. She was spunky. She was cute, and she seemed to be kinda hip.

Without even knowing what I was saying, I asked her, "So, will you disciple me? I just need a little-fine tuning, not a bunch of rearranging like my girlfriends. They are all *way* away from God. Me, though, my life's pretty much on track. I mean, it should be pretty easy to help me."

She stepped back and kinda checked me out. I don't know if she didn't think I was sincere or what, but the way she stared me up and down kinda freaked me out. *What was she thinking about?* I wondered. *What was going on in this lady's mind?* That's when I realized maybe I shouldn't have asked the question.

"So, you don't think you've had some crazy thoughts like your friends? Tell me about them."

I pretty much told her everything there was to know. Tad and her husband had strolled around the restaurant talking, so we just sat there and gabbed. It was easy for me to let loose and really let her totally into my world.

Shayna probed, "So um, you've told me about your friends and alcohol; do you drink? Do you want to? Prom's coming up; do you think you'll not want to make another toast? Then there's graduation. Yeah, let's not forget about graduation. You don't think you'll want to raise a glass or two to that big moment in your life? Then you mentioned another girlfriend wanting to or actually taking a puff. So you've never wondered what it feels like to be floating on a cloud, or drifting, as some people call it? You're better than that, right? Not even a hint of thinking about it? OK, maybe not that. That's understood; maybe you won't go there, but what about Tad? He's a cute brother. You don't imagine being with him physically? You know, like your other girl-friend wanting to be with her guy. What's her name? Rain. You don't have those feelings? You don't want to be with your guy?"

She was calling me out. I didn't really like it. I didn't

want to look deep within myself to see that I wasn't that far away from thinking the way my friends do. She was pretty tough on me, and those were just the surface questions. What happens when I have to answer them truthfully? Was I ready for someone to help me? Did I really want to go there? That next level in my relationship with Christ. Was I ready for someone discipling my life?

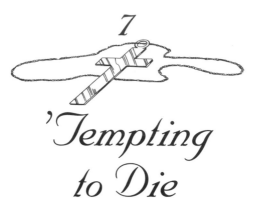

7

'Tempting to Die

I t seems that you don't like the tough questions," the sassy lady said to me.

Shayna Mullen was right. I was basically the same as my friends who I ridiculed. I too had impure thoughts. Impure thoughts themselves are sins, but I didn't know what to do about my lack of comfort. The situation wasn't easy. Someone picking me apart, telling me I was less than perfect. It bothered me.

In wisdom the thirty-year-old said, "Don't be so discouraged. We all fall short of the glory of God. I'm not asking you the tough questions because I myself am clean. I'm not throwing stones because I don't feel some could be thrown back at me. I'm not calling you out, my little sister, just for the heck of it. But I'm letting you see that sometimes we judge too harshly, and we shouldn't. Sometimes we accuse, and that's not right. Sometimes we got some of the same problems we find irritating in other people, and I just kinda wanted you to see that because I believe there's hope for you. So surely you gotta think there's hope for your friends."

Without even thinking, this lady had me hooked. She touched my shoulder and more wisdom came pouring from her mouth.

"The only way to do this is to let go of yourself and become more like Him, and that's a daily process. You seem like such a sweet girl, Payton. I'd be honored to be in your life and help you become the best you can be in Him, and it just takes commitment. So I want you to pray on it, and when you are ready to be discipled, come to me."

"You'll do great," I whispered to my brother's girlfriend before she entered the gym to tryout. As a senior cheerleader, I got a chance to train all the underclassmen trying out. She had what it took to make the varsity squad, and although I didn't give her extra attention because I thought everyone needed a chance, I definitely encouraged her that she could make the team. It appeared to me, as I looked in her eyes as she walked to try out, that she was timid, reserved, almost scared. I knew to make it, as in anything in life, you have to first believe you can before anyone else can see your confidence.

It always irritates me when people aren't prepared. Why would girls come to cheerleading tryouts with their lips poked out? They stand in front of the judges, looking as if they're mad at the world. They should be smiling and happy to cheer on their school's team. I could tell the girls that weren't going to make it. Not only did their faces appear to display anguish, but their appearance was not professional. I'm not saying they need to have new shoes, but their shirts should have been tucked in, and if you're trying out for cheerleading, goodness gracious, be able to do the splits, a cartwheel, jump . . . something.

I guess I should've been able to get it, but I finally realized that girls really want to fit in, that we want to belong. We want to be a part of what we perceive to be special. Even if we don't have the talent, we try to fit in. I don't have a problem with that necessarily, but I do have a problem with people not doing their homework. People not researching what a cheerleader is. Coming the week of tryouts and never a thought of taking gymnastics. It's as if they come expecting much more than a miracle.

Before tryouts started, there was a new part added to the judges' score sheet. It was the teacher's evaluation number. Out of five points, five being excellent, one being poor, teachers were able to rate the girls trying out. Just because of bad attitudes, most girls had a one.

"Tina," judge number one asked, "may I see your cheer?"

"GO! GO! GO! GO!"

All of a sudden Tina stopped doing the motion. Fear came over her face. She had lost it.

"Can I start over?" she said in a panic.

Judge number one said, "Yes you may."

I felt so bad for her. I could tell she couldn't regain her composure enough to do it over. Unfortunately, I was right. Tina fled past me, ran out the door, and started sobbing in the bathroom. Quickly I left the gym to follow her. Upon opening the door, I heard two girls that were next to try out start some drama.

"I told you she couldn't make it. She thinks she's so cute, but she doesn't have no spunk."

"I'm glad. We didn't want her to make it anyway."

When I heard the first comment, I wanted to turn around, but didn't. When I heard the second one, I had to turn around.

"Why you tryin' to keep down your peers? With talk like that, you better hope you make it."

"Hey, you heard us? We were just playin'. We weren't really serious. We're just teasin'," one of the girls tried to play it off.

"I hope so, because if you were in that situation you sure wouldn't want someone to take pleasure in your down time."

She was squatted in the corner of the bathroom when I found her. Such a pitiful creature. I had no idea what to say. I realized by caring for a girl just three years younger than I how much she respected who I was as a senior. So I proceeded to encourage her. I stooped over and touched her shoulder.

"Don't give up. Don't quit. Don't not try."

"But I walked out, Payton. I walked out. Surely I wouldn't get another try," she rationalized.

"I'll ask Coach to let you try again. I can get you another chance before the judges, but only you can make the squad."

About an hour after tryouts, the cheerleading list was posted. I was so hoping my brother's friend would make it. Needless to say, I was ecstatic to see the letters T-I-N-A!

When I got home Perry was anxiously awaiting my arrival. Never before had he greeted me with such niceness. I had to mess with him.

With a dejected look, I said, "You better go call yo' girl!"

"Daaang! She wanted to make it really bad too," Perry voiced in despair. "What can I say to her, Pay? I want to be sensitive and all."

Nonchalantly I uttered, "Tell her congratulations."

"SHE MADE IT!" Perry screamed. "Ya know you wrong!"

Hugging my brother made me very happy. He thanked me for helping Tina. That gesture made me even happier. Perry had been there for me so many times. I was glad I could finally be there for him.

Although a week had passed in school, my friendship with Dymond, Lynzi, and Rain was still strained. Actually it was quite petty. They weren't talking to me. I wasn't talking to them. That day seeing a ninth grader, whose peers didn't want her to succeed and me charging them to support her, made me know that I needed to support my own peers. I needed to mend the fences with my friends. I needed to make peace.

I drove up to Rain's house and was excited to see her car there. Her mom let me in and I headed up to her room.

God wants us to forgive. Satan, on the other hand, comes to destroy. I wanted God to be victorious in every part of my life. For Him to win in this area, I had to forgive.

She looked up at me and yelled, "Oh no. I have absolutely nothing to say to you, Payton Skky. Get out!"

"I'm not saying I owe you an apology, but I'm definitely not leaving either."

"If you ain't leaving, I'm getting out of here."

"See, why it got to be like that? Why you gotta act like that? I miss our friendship; can't we put all differences aside?" I asked her honestly.

"Yeah, right. You just miss dictating," she told me bluntly.

Maybe she was right. I hoped she wasn't, but I knew, although I was still angry, I did want to be around her.

"Why you trying to kill our friendship? Why don't you at least wanna try? Why don't you want what we used to have? Why you actin' like that? You know what? I don't even want to be here. I don't even have to go through this with you. I don't know why I came here anyway," I turned around and left.

Before I could get out of the house, I was detained.

Dymond rushed in. She was in a panic.

Dymond enforced, "Ya'll come on. Come on, ya'll. Come on. Lynzi is trippin'."

"What are you talking about?" Rain questioned. "Calm down."

"No, I'm serious." Dymond then broke down and said with emotion, "She left the craziest message on my machine. She said she followed Bam last night. She said she went to Bam's house last night to give another plea that he would stay with her and used the key he gave her to sneak into his place late at night."

"Slow down," I asked. "You're not making sense. What do you mean, she snuck into his place late at night?"

"'Cause you know his mama work late at night. Lynzi might never have told ya'll, but she used to go up over there. Well, she used the key and instead of surprising him, she got surprised. Somebody was already occupying that bed with the brother, and the whole experience has made her not want to go on. I don't know where to find her. I don't know where she is. I don't know what she's doing. I just know—ya'll, I'm serious—she's 'tempting to die."

8

Crashing Downhill

*I*nside I felt numb. I didn't know what to think. This was pretty scary, but surely it couldn't be true.

Rushing out of Rain's house, my mind wasn't with me. I turned around and slammed straight into the door. It wasn't just a slight bump; it was a big one. One that hurt dramatically. Rain had already grabbed her keys and got in her car, and so had Dymond. After I had slightly stopped hurting, I rushed out as well. Why we all got in three different cars was absolutely beyond me, but we did anyway.

I pulled out of the driveway and waited for Dymond to lead. Rain pulled out of her driveway the same time Dy pulled forward. Rain slammed into the front of Dymond's car. They were both moving at the same time. No one was hurt, but it further depressed us. We didn't even have time to see the damage of their cars. They just parked, got out and got in the car with me.

"Ya'll think she's OK?" I asked as we drove a little farther out of the neighborhood.

"I don't know. I don't know," Dymond said hastily. "But I know that she didn't sound good, and anything could be happening. I think she was drinkin'"

Rain was looking out the window with not a word to say.

"Now, I know you ain't still mad at me," I quizzed in disbelief. "There's a lot going on with our friend. We need to at least come together and put our differences aside, so that we can try and find Lynzi."

"Oh, so now you trying to use what's going on with our friend to make *our* friendship work? I don't even think so. It's not that simple, Payton."

Dymond entered the conversation and said, "Maybe she's right, Rain."

"Nahh, don't try and tell her I'm right, Dymond. She got an attitude, then she can get out of my car and walk. Shoot, I don't have time for this drama either."

I stopped the car, pulled the car over and said, "Get out! Get out!"

"Fine," she stood up and slammed my door.

Boy, did I want to hit her. Rain started to walk away. I didn't care at that point. I was too angry to beg somebody to come back. As I started to take off and drive right past her, Dymond opened the car door.

"What are you doing?" I said. "It's dangerous."

"I'm sick of the two of ya'll. Stop the car. I'm sick of the two of ya'll."

I stopped, not because I wanted to, but because if I didn't I'd probably run over Dymond. At that point, it seemed Dymond was the only one who cared about keeping our friendship together. I was through with it all. I had reached the boiling point. I noticed Rain continued to walk back to her house. She didn't care about us being of one accord either. Dymond went over to her, pulled her arm, and pushed her into the backseat of my Jeep. I was happy when the cell phone rang. By answering it, I wouldn't have to entertain talking to the two of them. It was really awkward, the atmosphere in my ride. However, because we were concerned about finding Lynzi, there was an unspoken agreement to work as a team.

"This is probably her right now," I hoped.

"Hello?"

"Payton."

"Lynzi!" I shouted out, "Girl, where are you? Where are you?"

"You didn't return my phone calls this week, Payton."

"I'm so sorry. I'm so sorry I didn't return your calls."

"You don't have to worry about returning them anymore. I was just calling to tell you goodbye," Lynzi said in a depressed voice.

"Lynz—Lynz—Lynz—No! No! No! Don't talk like that. Where are you? Where are you? I'm with Rain and Dymond and we're coming to get you. Lynzi, please, tell me where you are," I begged.

Dymond wanted to grab the phone away and talk to her. However, I pushed her hand back because I needed to continue to speak to my friend who did not sound like herself. I needed to try and give her some type of hope. I needed her to see that God had a purpose and a plan for her life, and she was not to end it.

"I'm hanging up now, Payton."

"No! No! Don't hang up. Lynzi, please don't hang up."

"I've been a bad girl, Payton. You told me not to drink anymore. My mom is gonna be so mad that I took her vodka, scotch, and some of that other stuff. Three bottles. I only have one more to go."

"She's drunk," I mouthed to Rain and Dymond as they listened intently to try and help me figure what was going on.

"I hope you're not driving. Please Lynzi, tell me where

you are."

"I don't know . . . where I am. Don't know where I'm at. I know I won't be anywhere real soon. I'm leavin'. Somebody once told me that black folks don't kill themselves. Ha! I'll be able to tell them that they're wrong. 'Cause I'm gonna kill myself. But if I've died, I guess I can't tell them. Will you tell them for me, Payton?"

Emotionally it hit me. For the first time, I realized Lynzi was hurting so bad that she didn't want to hurt anymore. The only option she felt was not to be here. How could I help her feel like something? How could I make her see we cared? How could I make her want to go on?

As a tear streamed from my face, I screamed, "No, Lynzi! Don't do it! Don't drive! Don't go! Wait on us. Let us help you. Please, Lynzi, please. Please let me get there. I know it hurts, but it won't hurt forever. You'll get over it. You'll be OK."

I heard her car start up. My heart was beating faster than a race car driver drives. *Cut off the car,* I thought.

"Oh no!" I exclaimed when I realized her car wasn't cutting off.

"Well, I'll see ya. Ya'll take care of each other. Whew," Lynzi let out before hanging up.

Silence. Nothing. The phone went dead.

"Oh my gosh, ya'll. She's serious," I told them.

Rain started praying, "Heavenly Father, help our friend. We don't know where she is. We don't know what she's doing. We just know she hurts. She needs You. We need You. Let her be OK. In Jesus' name, Amen."

"I don't know where to go. Where should I start looking? She could be anywhere."

"Well, let's just drive over to her house. Maybe she's on her way home or something. Maybe she—" Rain started to cry.

This was hard. My tenacious friend, Lynzi, should never

be in this situation. No person, especially a young person, should ever feel like life is too heavy to keep carrying on. Then we all started the "I should have" conversation. I felt I should have returned her calls. Rain felt she should not have been so mad at her over the whole Tyson incident. Dymond felt she should have taken her more seriously when she mentioned suicide a week ago.

Dymond said in a depressed tone, "I just thought she was kidding, so I kidded back with her. I just said, 'Well, girl, yeah, it might just be the best thing. At least you don't have to deal with the craziness. Yeah, go and kill yourself.' I never knew she was serious. Lord, forgive me."

I grabbed her hand and said, "We'll find her. We all now know how much we do need each other." I turned and looked at Rain and said, "So I'm sorry for coming down so hard on you for your feelings for your guy. I dreamed about Tad last night. I thought how neat it would be to feel his body up next to mine. Although it was a brief, quick thought, and I dismissed it instantly knowing that that wasn't going to happen until he was my husband, I went there. So, I now understand why you're there, and I'm sorry for not understanding it sooner."

"You were right to talk me out of it. I would've regretted it, had I done it. I was just too prideful to tell you, but I thank you for knocking some sense into me. I want God to be proud of my daily relationship, and I want friends like you who care more than I want you to. Friends who stick their noses way too far into my business. Friends who go the extra mile to stop me from doing something stupid. Thank you."

We had been driving around for two hours, with no more calls from Lynzi, and no calls from anyone saying where she was. Panic had overtaken the three of us. We were in a predicament worse than that.

"Ya'll hungry?" I asked.

Although my stomach was in knots and I couldn't eat, I at least wanted to be sympathetic to the fact that maybe they could.

"Girl, I can't eat a thing," Dymond, my friend who never passes up food, said.

"I can't eat either," Rain commented from the back.

"Where is she?" I let out in despair.

"That girl kno' she wrong for this. We love her. That stupid Bam. I wish I could beat him up myself."

"Me and Fatz are cool. I love him, but I ain't gon' let him get in my mind so much that if he walks away I can't go on. Forget that. That's crazy," Dymond preached. "I know ya'll in love and stuff, but shoot, we should love God more than any man. He doesn't want us to kill ourselves."

"I know that's right," I agreed.

Rain asked, "What is all that noise?"

"Fire trucks and ambulances, I think," I answered.

I was right, we found out. We had to pull over to the side of the road to let four emergency vehicles pass us. The noise was frightening.

"I hope that person's all right," I uttered with concern.

Dymond said, "Yeah, me too. We just need to find Lynzi so that won't be her."

"Let's call her mom," Rain suggested.

Dy explained, "Naw, we don't want to upset her. Plus we should keep the line open for Lynzi."

"You have call waiting, don't you, Payton?" Rain asked.

Quickly I said, "Yes, but while I dial out the line would be busy. We'll call in a while."

We drove another mile down the street. When we went around a two-lane, curvy road, we saw a horrible sight. There were even more red sirens going off there.

"What's goin' on?" Rain cried.

"Oh my gosh . . . I hope that's not—" I couldn't fully get my words out.

I gripped Dymond's hand, and that's when Rain said, "Ya'll, I think it is, 'cause there's her mom's car."

Quickly, we pulled over to the side and hopped out of my car. Rain and Dymond were too scared to move. I ran down the embankment and screamed when I saw my friend's car wrapped around a tree.

As I tried to go closer the police said, "Stay back. Stay back. We're trying to pry the car loose."

I heard Dymond's sobs, as we knew Lynzi was in deep trouble. To the eye, it seemed like God took her home, but in my heart I still believed she was with us.

"What happened to her? What happened?" I cried out for answers. "Please tell me what happened."

With a solemn voice the officer replied, "We haven't pieced together the details. We just know her car went crashing downhill."

9

Waiting with Expectation

"We've got a pulse, sir," one of the medics said to the police officer.

"Hurry! Hurry! We've got to get this young lady out of this car. She is still alive," the other person working on Lynzi replied intensely.

My parents had come and so had Dakari. There were actually about fifty or so people praying that Lynzi would be OK. When Dymond noticed Bam, she just lost it.

"How dare you come here. How dare you show your face. If it wasn't for you, everybody wouldn't be here watching. Why don't you just go. Nobody wants you here. Leave!"

Dymond started pounding on him, trying to get him to leave, and shouted, "Go! Go!"

Rain and I went over to her and tried to calm her down. However, she was too furious to be cool. Part of me agreed with her anger, although it wouldn't do us any good to harbor it.

Dakari went over to Bam and said, "Man, maybe you

better leave."

While Fatz drove off with Bam, Dakari hung around. I didn't know where Tad was. I tried to call him and left several messages with his mom. I needed him right now. I needed him to keep me strong. As I saw the awful condition of Lynzi's car, I didn't know how much longer I could stay positive for myself, for my two friends, or for poor Lynzi.

"Her legs are stuck. Her legs are stuck," the emergency guy yelled in a panicky voice.

"I can't move her," the other medic attested. "I can't move her."

The police officer questioned, "Is she conscious?"

"No, she is not conscious, but she is alive, sir."

"What's going on?" Lynzi's mom screamed as she almost passed out.

I rushed over to Dakari. At that moment, it was as if he meant as much to me as he always had. In the midst of the confusion and uncertainty, I was glad to see his face.

I whimpered to him, "I'm so scared for my friend. I'm so scared."

He held me in his arms and cried, "Don't stop believing. She's gonna be OK. She's gonna be OK. She's gonna be OK."

Lynzi's mom must have called Lynzi's dad right away. Although he lived in Atlanta, he drove right up to the scene. When they finally got Lynzi out, there was blood on the lower part of her body. It was a horrifying sight.

Being wrapped in Dakari's secure embrace was comforting. So comforting that the chaos around me, the horror around me, the pain around me didn't feel so bad. Unfortunately, the reality still existed.

"Thank you," I said to my ex-boyfriend as he calmed me down and held me together. "Thank you for being here. Thank you for caring. Thank you for saying she'll be alright. I hope so. I hope so."

He clenched my hand and would not let me go as we

watched in sadness as the ambulance passed us by. Lynzi's mother was physically OK. We were all glad for that. Though we wanted to go to the hospital, Lynzi's parents thought we should go home. It would be easier that way. Rain and Dymond took my keys and headed to my car to wait on me. Dakari, still holding my hand, walked me up the hill to my Jeep.

He asked me, with passion, "You sure you're gonna be OK? I can follow you home."

A voice from behind cut in. "She'll be fine. I'll follow her home. Thanks, but no thanks."

It was Tad. Immediately I let go of Dakari's hand and went over to the arms of my beau. I saw dejection in Dakari's face, but it really didn't sink in how disappointed he was that I left and went to my guy. I sensed, also, that Tad was a bit bummed out that I was being comforted by Dakari, but their feelings didn't matter. All that really mattered was that my good friend was in a bad condition and on her way to the hospital.

Tad kept his word. After taking home my girlfriends, he followed me to my place. I was glad he was behind me. I needed to vent.

I explained as we stood in the driveway, "I know this is wrong, but I'm angry at God. I don't even know if she's going to be OK, and judging from the way her legs looked, she might not even walk again. It just doesn't seem right. I just can't understand why God would allow this to happen. We prayed. Didn't He hear us, Tad? Didn't He hear our prayer? She didn't even make it home to sleep all that alcohol off. He should've got her home. God doesn't care."

"Alcohol? She'd been drinking?" he probed.

I knew I shouldn't have opened my big mouth. We had vowed not to drink anymore because it could potentially cause an accident. Although alcohol is what led my friend, Lynzi, into this mess, no one needed to know it, but now I had just told Tad.

"Yeah, she'd been drinking, but she was really mentally messed up. She didn't even want to go on. I just thought God cared and that He would just help her and stuff. None of this should have happened. I mean, what kind of God do we serve? Dymond, Rain, and I linked and prayed, and I just don't understand," I explained.

"I'm not trying to preach to you. I feel what you're saying, but I can't let you be so mad at God that you think He really doesn't care. He does hear."

"Yeah, right! Don't even try that junk with me. If He heard me, she wouldn't have hit a tree. If He heard me, she wouldn't be in the hospital holding on for dear life."

Wisely he told me, "She took herself out of God's grace with her own sin. It's not your fault. You prayed, right? It's not God's fault either."

"I can't feel anything," Lynzi said two days later when she wasn't under so much medication and could comprehend her present state.

"Just relax," the nurse told her. "Just relax."

Her legs were crushed and all bandaged up, and the doctors were afraid she would be paralyzed. No one knew how to break the news to her, and I was still too angry to pray and ask God for help when I already felt He had betrayed us.

"You don't understand," Lynzi ranted. "I can't feel my legs. I . . . I can't feel my legs. What . . . what's wrong? Ma, what's wrong? I can't feel my legs."

Lynzi's dad said, "Lynzi, you gotta be tough, honey. You gotta relax. You gotta be smart about all of this. Getting upset isn't gonna help your cause. You've done enough already. And don't baby her, Lexi."

"Listen, this is my daughter," Lynzi's mom said to him.

"Don't tell me how to raise my child. Don't tell me how to comfort her when she's obviously in pain. I need to be here for her. If you have a problem with our affection, then *leave* the room."

I couldn't believe I was standing in the hospital room hearing all this. They were having a family discussion, and I didn't know whether it'd be rude to leave or rude to stay, so in my position, I froze.

Mr. Green lashed out, "She wouldn't be drinking if it wasn't for you. You let her drink at the house like she was some kind of an adult or something. Then she drinks all the stuff you got lying around. Now look at her; she's ended up here."

"Me?" her mother retorted back. "She always talks about how her father doesn't care for her. She wouldn't be trying to have a boyfriend so bad if she felt that affection from you."

"Both of you are right, so just shut up, please. Just shut up all the screaming and the yelling. Please. Please," Lynzi voiced, all upset.

Lynzi had always put up a good front, saying that being a product of a broken home was no big deal. She said she was fine just like everybody else. Said she had no scars, no hurt, and no pain. It was obvious to her parents, as well as to me, that that was a front she could no longer hold up. The decision they made to walk away from their marriage had affected their daughter and probably would for the rest of her life.

At that very moment, I promised myself that if the Lord ever saw fit for me to be someone's bride, I would make sure I wanted to love that person for the rest of my life. That I wanted to give everything to that man. That I wanted to make it work even if things got crazy, and that if we were blessed with children, they would know our bond was solid. That their foundation was the Rock—Jesus Christ.

85

They would never be abandoned.

Her two parents could do nothing but go up and hug her. In the warmth of their moment, I knew then they needed privacy. I softly exited and met up with my mom to go look for prom dresses.

"I don't like this one, Mom," I uttered in frustration at the mall.

"Payton, what's wrong with this dress? It's cute and adorable. I'm not buying you some slim something for you to go parading around here in."

"Ma, I didn't say I wanted somethin' like that. I just don't want this one."

"Oooh, what about this?" my mother asked

My mom and I had been shopping for about three hours. Store to store. Mall to mall. Nothing. Nothing caught my eye. We parted ways after lunch. She said she'd keep looking. Those words sent chills up my spine, because everything she picked out was hideous. No way I'd want to go to Tad's prom looking like a fifth-grader, as opposed to an elegant lady of grace. Mom said she knew what I was looking for. I said OK and we parted ways.

I just couldn't get Lynzi out of my mind. A friend of mine not wanting to be around. I must've not done my job as a buddy. I knew I'd dropped the ball, and since I had another chance, although I might not get her to walk again, surely I could lift her spirits. *Keep her encouraged,* I thought, but how was I gonna do that? Shucks, even I myself was kinda bummed out about the whole thing.

When I entered the hospital room, she was there with a guest I didn't want to see. It was Bam. Bam! Bam! Bam!

"Hey, Lynzi," I said, keeping my cool as I leaned over and kissed her on the cheek.

"Could you excuse us, Bam?" I said to him, trying to

contain any ounce of frustration.

He let go of her hand and exited the room. I was furious. He was not what she needed to end the cycle of depression. I was afraid. Really afraid for her to have any type of correspondence with this guy.

"What's wrong with you? I can tell you're kinda mad. I know you. What's up?" Lynzi, being real, asked.

I appreciated her stepping up to the plate and calling me out because yes, a lot of things were going on and I was a pretty unhappy person. I didn't know if I could be real back. I didn't know if I could tell her what I was really feeling. Here I am, a person that's trying to get her to walk closer to God, and I felt so far from Him. A hypocrite. Yeah, that's kinda what I felt like.

"You're angry."

"Yes, I'm angry. God . . . I don't know where He is. I feel like I'm falling apart and tearing in a million pieces. It seems like my life is being squeezed right out of me. I have nothing to hope in. I don't even feel like I can win. I guess I kinda thought you were crazy for feeling like you felt a couple of days ago, and now I kinda feel like that. I prayed for God to help you and He didn't. He didn't! What . . . what kinda God would allow you to sit there and be here like this? I don't know."

"Payton, God did help me. I couldn't tell you earlier 'cause of all the stuff going on with my parents. God saved my life. He spared me. I was so out of it. I don't remember much. I just remember closing my eyes in the middle of the street because the alcohol had consumed me, and I said, 'Lord, I'm sorry. I want to live. Help me!' And I hit a tree. I hit a tree instead of a person. I hit the tree just the right way that if I would have hit it an inch to the left or to the right, I would've been gone. God heard your prayer, my friend. You stood on His Word and it worked for me. He covered me with His grace. Listen to this song."

She turned around and raised the volume on her CD player. She was playing a Fred Hammond song, and the words that I remember said, "All things are working for me. Even things I can't see."

Hearing Lynzi say that God did answer our prayers was so awesome. I just didn't want her to crash. I didn't want her to die. I was so encouraged by her spunk for life and her zeal for life. Her zest for life. God didn't lie. We called on Him, and He was there once again. All I could do was shed a tear for not having enough faith to believe that He'd do that in the first place.

"OK, I'm sitting here. Tell me what's up with that guy," I asked as I pointed to the door.

"Bam?"

"Yes, Bam."

"I love him. Am I trying to walk down that same road? No. I don't know; it's like God told me I need Jesus, but that still doesn't mean I can't help Bam find the same God. Of course he feels bad, sorry, all that stuff, and when I hit the tree, I wasn't trying to kill myself anymore. God had already cured me of that hurt and that pain. So I can look at Bam and everything he's put me through and, yes, be disappointed, and yes, not want it to happen again, but no, not not have him in my life. I don't want anything from him, and therefore I can't be hurt. I enjoy his company, Payton, but I won't be his girlfriend. I have learned my lesson with the triflin' brother. And things are going to be better, because now I'm in control of my own feelings. So get on out of here, girl. You got a prom to go to tomorrow."

"I guess I do. It's weird 'cause Tad never said we weren't going to his prom, but he never said we were either. With everything going on . . . I don't know. I guess it's just as well. I haven't even found a dress anyway. Alright, I love you, girl. And again, I'm so sorry for not being there for you."

"You got my back now?" Lynzi teased.

Smiling, I replied, "Yeah, I got your back."

As soon as I got in my room, my telephone rang. Picking it up, I was glad to hear Tad's voice. With joy, I told him about my day.

"Heeyyy! My spirits are a little better. My friend, Lynzi, helped me put things back in perspective. So what's going on?" I said.

"My mom got on me because I didn't handle my business the way I should have."

"What do you mean?" I pried.

"Well, my coach, the one that's discipling me, Coach Mullen, along with some of the press, really want some footage of me at the prom, and I guess even above that, I want to take my girlfriend on my arms to my school. Show my friends how proud I am that you're my girl. I wanted to ask you at your house a while ago over dinner, but we never got back to it. I don't even know when your prom is. Mine is—"

"Yours is tomorrow," I said, cutting him off.

"How'd you know?"

"Research."

"Is it like . . . too late for you to maybe go with me?"

"So are you asking me now?"

"Help a brother out. Yes, I'm asking you. Payton Skky, will you be my date for the prom tomorrow night? It'd probably make my senior year."

"Well, I surely can't let you down. What time will you be here to pick me up?"

"Six."

"I'll be ready."

"I'm sure you'll be more than ready. I'm sure you'll be beautiful," Tad sweetly talked.

Hanging up the phone, I sat down on my bed thinking,

Beautiful, yeah, right. I have nothing to wear. Then I realized I was sitting on something. It was a box smashed in from the imprint I'd just made. I opened it up and pulled out the most gorgeous fuscia gown. It was everything and more that I was looking for. It was so pretty.

My mom peeped in the door and said, "I thought that this would look gorgeous on you. Is this what you had in mind?"

I couldn't say or do anything but rush up to her, with the dress in hand, and give her the biggest hug she'd had in a while. In my mother's arms, I was happier than I'd been in a long time. I had a date to the prom and a beautiful dress to wear. My friend helped me see something very important: Jesus is there and He still cares. The answers I'd been longing to find, I had them. I was at peace. I was no longer waiting with expectation.

10

Acting for Him

"Why today?" I wondered aloud as I felt a cramp and looked at my calendar.

I said with sarcasm, "Yep, it's that time again. Just great."

I had spent all day working on the final touches. I had gone to the hairdresser. I had gotten my nails done. I had shopped for just the right perfume. Although I had taken Midol, I felt horrible. When he came to the door, though, the gorgeous gentleman before me in that striking black tuxedo made some of that pain disappear. Kissing me on the cheek and giving me a corsage, he warmed my heart. He was fine, and he was mine. He was my date for the evening, and he was my man. Period. The end!

Though this wasn't my school, I knew I would have to watch for some crazy sisters trying to step out of line and disrespect me. I was ready for them though, and I knew I especially was gonna have to watch that one girl that's always had the hots for him. Hopefully, though, the night would be fun. Although I felt horrible, I was ready to step out with him.

"How do you feel?" he asked me.

"Great," I answered untruthfully, but hoping to start our night off with a bang.

He said he couldn't get a limousine 'cause he waited 'til the last minute, but his uncle did allow him to drive his Cadillac. That was really nice. Tad had the ride looking and smelling good.

We got to his prom, which was in his school gym. Not my first choice, but to my surprise, it was beautifully decorated in a Hawaiian motif. I went to the table and sat down, thinking my date would be joining me, but he got called in several different directions. So for the first forty minutes or so, I was alone.

Two guys strolled up to me. They had been checkin' me out for a while.

"Heeyyy, beautiful lady. Shame on your date for leaving something as delicious as you alone at the table. Look at the watermelon in that dress."

I was hoping he didn't think his line was cute, because it was quite irritating. Something about the guy was familiar to me. I couldn't place it.

To keep from them being embarrassed, the other guy came to the rescue and said, "Forget my friend. He's trippin'! In his own weird way he was trying to say you're absolutely breathtaking. May I have this dance?"

I had been sittin' there forever. I hoped Tad wouldn't be mad if I danced with somebody. Was I not going to show off my pumps, my dress, my hair, or those nails? I couldn't sit there all night long. I wasn't mad that he had to tend to what he had to take care of, but for sure I wasn't going to sit, sit, sit.

"So where are your dates?" I asked the guy that was swaying me back and forth.

"We came stag. Most of the people in our school do. I

guess a lot of folks are surprised your boy brought you."

"Well, I hope they're not disappointed."

"I'm not. 'Cause if he didn't bring you, I wouldn't have got to view such a vision. I ain't trying to come on, but you fine."

"I got it bro', thanks," Tad cut in and said.

"Oh, all right. I'm just keepin' your lady occupied while you do yo thang."

"Well, I'm done. Thanks. You can take your seat, drink some punch, dance with somebody else, whatever."

"Are you jealous, Tad Taylor? That's the second time somebody's had your lady's other hand and you've cut in and said I've got it. You know I'm yours, right? There are no insecurities floatin' around in that head of yours, are there? Talk to me. What's up?"

"Dakari told me himself that he wants you," Tad started explaining with a stern voice. "Told me himself, OK? If you don't think he does, that's cool, but he told me. I just always need the guys to know that you are my girl, and that's not up for grabs. They need to understand, and every chance I get I'll tell them. It has nothing to do with jealousy. It has everything to do with strength, and that dude that was just over here, him and his partners over there, they didn't even want me to get into Georgia. They been playa' hatin' for years. Folks like that—folks you don't trust, you surely ain't gon' trust them around your woman. Uh-uh! That's out. No!"

"Yeah," I sarcastically said with a smile. "Oh, I remember them now. They came to that announcement of your signing you had here. Yeah, I remember. I thought I knew them."

"I do have some friends here if you wanna dance with someone other than me," he joked as he pulled away to leave my side.

I reached out and pulled him back as a slow song played

over the loudspeakers. I was feeling wonderful. With his arms wrapped around me, it was easy to want to be no place else other than right where I was.

In the ladies' room a little later on, I ran into the chick that liked Tad a lot. I always forget her name, but her face, that sly, slick face, I couldn't forget. Even though she was a debutante with me and we should be nice, I knew she had something on her mind that wasn't nice at all. So I tried to ignore her 'cause I didn't want a confrontation. I was with Tad, and I wasn't trying to cause a scene.

"We are so sorry. We are so sorry," she overdramatized. "We heard your girlfriend tried to kill herself. That . . . that girl Lynzi. She is your girlfriend, isn't she? Oh my gosh, the poor thing. Someone said she still might die. That's a shame that your friend would want to take her own life. I am so sorry to hear that. Surely you couldn't have been anywhere around or you would have tried to stop her, right? Maybe you were with Tad or something? I hope she's OK. Where were you?"

So many things ran through my body. How could people be so insensitive and so cold? This girl had an attitude because the guy she liked, liked me. Get over it. What was going on with Lynzi is serious stuff. To be sarcastic made me want to claw into her, but that's not the Christian attitude. God didn't want me to act like a fool. And I was with Tad. I had to show this nut why Tad chose me instead of her.

So I turned to her and said, "My friend is OK. God's got her in His hand. Good night."

When I came out of the bathroom, Tad was standing there waiting for me. He reached his arms out and gave me a hug as if he knew I needed it. Surely he didn't, but I was so glad he was there to embrace me.

Before I pulled away, the girl came out with her friend. "Oh Tad! Hey, babe. You look so handsome."

"Doesn't my man look good?" I said exercising my turn

to be sarcastic.

The girl looked at me with disgust. She rudely tried cutting in between us. However, Tad wasn't letting go of the grip.

"I know you gon' save a dance for me. Dancin' with me will surely be the highlight of your evening. You ain't gon' keep him all night, are you honey?"

I looked at him and waited for him to answer. I didn't want to get in it, but if he wouldn't set her straight then I would.

Tad gracefully declined. "Sorry, I've gotta dance with my girl. No dances with anyone but her. Ya'll have a good time though. See ya'll Monday."

The time was special because Tad made me feel special. Dinner was special because he spared no expense on treating me like a lady all the while we dined. Before taking me home, he took me to a quiet spot, and we gazed up at the stars. It was such a beautiful night in Aiken, South Carolina. I had taken my shoes off and he plopped me on the hood of his uncle's car.

He was standing up right beside me and said, "I love you."

Then out of the blue he gave me a kiss. It was sweeter than a strawberry in season. The kiss was definitely passionate.

The kiss wasn't as innocent as it maybe should have been. As it definitely should have been. It was much, much more. It was warm and inviting. It was as if it was asking me to do much, much more. Feeling the energy made me want to do more.

Tad didn't stop at one kiss. He came at me again. This time it was longer, and even harder to break away from. However, I did.

"We can't," I abruptly pulled away from his caressing

grip and said. "We can't!"

Though deep down I wanted to keep going, I played it off. I fronted like being that close to him was the last thing on my mind. I knew heaven was pleased with me for stopping the moment. Deep down it was a small applause, because I knew that God knew that I was acting for Him.

11

Facing My Fears

"Oh my gosh," I said in despair as my mom called me into the family room and I learned of the tragic news.

Four high school seniors, all girls, died in a car accident. Celebrating the beginning had turned into their end. Although I didn't have all the details, early reports said alcohol was involved. My heart sunk deeper than the bottomless pit of the Pacific Ocean. I shared their families' pain.

Then reality hit. It could have easily been me. Me riding with my three best friends. We were ready to get out and enjoy life. We were ready to celebrate our accomplishments. We were ready to be out there and not really care about the consequences. And for those four girls, it was too late. How final, I thought. Yet, unfortunately, those girls could not turn back the hands of time.

Would I take their story and learn from it, or would I allow circumstances and peer pressure to make their story my own? As the situation was too close to home, I shed tears of sorrow. My mother left the couch and stood beside me. Her embrace was more than comforting. It was as if she was showing me she understood and cared about what I was going through.

"Mommy, that's so sad," I uttered with tears. "It's so sad."

"I know, baby, but even though it doesn't seem like it, God still has a plan, and I know He wants you to learn from this incident. You hear me, baby? Learn."

Later that afternoon, Lynzi was due to be released from the hospital. She was doing remarkably better. Rain, Dymond and I went over to share in her excitement. Lynzi's mom was outside signing all the papers. The four of us were talking about the events that took place that morning. We discussed in detail the deadly tragedy. It seemed weird talking about it with them, my three friends, my best buddies, my hang-out partners. Yet, there were four girls our age lying without a breath in them. I knew if it wasn't for the grace of God it could have been all four of us instead of those four precious souls that have now gone on.

"I just wonder what happened. I mean, it was raining last night, but dang, they should've been more careful," Dymond said with little compassion.

Lynzi voiced, "Yeah, I hate that they won't get to do hardly anything else. That is so sad. But we gotta believe they're better off."

"'Hardly anything else'? They're dead. What are you talking about?" Rain uttered to Lynzi.

"Well, I mean, what we think is good may not be necessarily how God views it. Surely they're in a better place," Lynzi told them with shaky confidence.

"Are you just saying this 'cause you wanted to kill yourself?" Dymond asked her.

"No . . . no, I mean, go with me for a minute. Hold on! Don't interrupt. Let me say this right," Lynzi said.

But she didn't have to say a word. I knew what she meant. I knew what she was trying to say, but desperately having a hard time saying it.

Lynzi spoke wisely, "Like Paul says in the Word, 'It's far better for me not to be in this miserable life.' Although graduation and college is exciting and the rest of our lives are ahead of us, heaven is still a much better place. After all, eyes haven't seen the wonderful place God prepared for those who love Him. I just hoped they loved Him."

"Let's not talk about them. It's making me sad. I wanna know how this girl is walking. You beat the odds, girl," I told my friend who now possessed a stride better than mine.

"I guess I just quit being scared and I just prayed," Lynzi told me. "The next thing I knew, the swelling went down. God heard me. I got up and fell a couple of times, but I tried and tried again. I knew He had my steps, and I knew He had a direction for me to walk, and I knew the only way I could go that way was to get up. Rise up. Take up my bed. And so I walked."

"Girl, quit preachin'," Dymond said as she nudged our friend.

"That is so sweet," I said to her, almost teary, but still definitely riding on the emotion about the girls in Jackson, South Carolina.

I had to dig deep and open up to the young ladies who meant so much to me. I had to display my feelings like a blooming onion. I needed to be real. Life is not guaranteed, so I had to seize the moment.

"I just want to say I love you guys. I'm not trying to be all weird or anything, but we always go through stuff, and sometimes we go through it apart. The reason why we have each other is so we can go through things together. It's so we can help each other face stuff that's kinda crazy. I just wanna let ya'll know I'm here forever. I'm here for life, and if you need me, just give me a call and I'll answer."

We all hugged, and the embrace felt magnificent. I loved my friends, and being in that hospital room rejoicing instead of mourning made me feel good.

I was awakened that next morning by my mother. Although it was Sunday, it was too early to be trying to go to church. Surely that was not what she was waking me up for.

"It's your grandfather. We have to go to Conyers. Payton, sweetie, get up. He had a stroke."

This just couldn't be happening. My Pa Pa sick? No way! He had been my anchor my whole life. A Baptist preacher, who sent me calendars all my life on Scriptures to carry me through the day. Him, suffering? I couldn't imagine it. Having pain? No way! A stroke? I thought, *Lord help my family. Be with my grandfather, and keep my grandma calm.*

"Hold on, Pa Pa," I said as I got dressed. "Help is on the way."

The trip was less than two hours. However, it felt like an eternity. We had to go from my home to Rockdale County Hospital. Everyone couldn't go in, so Perry and I had to peep at my grandfather hooked up to all those machines through the window. The one I'd always known to possess strength looked weak. It was a distressing sight.

"God, you gotta help me out here," I said to myself. "We are trying to believe, but it's hard. One blow after another. I'm just tired. I'm so tired. I'm so young, but I don't think I can take it anymore. My friends, strangers, my grandfather . . . just suffering. Make it go away, dear Lord."

After talking to the doctor, my parents came out. I couldn't read their faces. I could only pray that the outcome would not be grave.

"Pa Pa gon' be okay? Tell me what's wrong. Say something," I bombarded them with questions.

"The doctor doesn't have any answers for us yet. We just gotta wait and pray," my dad voiced sternly, but you could see how much in agony he was over the situation.

Several grim faces filled my grandparents' house. I was hoping even in the midst of facts Pa Pa would pull through. My dad was the second child of five boys, and my family was the closest in proximity. So I felt my parents weren't telling me everything when I started seeing all my uncles take up the space in their home. Before the day had ended, family flew in from everywhere. I was especially surprised when Uncle Percy, my dad's oldest brother, walked into the room. He never comes home. Ever since he entered into an interracial marriage, his relationship with our family was strained. He wasn't alone. My cousin, Pillar, was with him.

All of sudden my body got cold. Heavenly thoughts, good thoughts, pleasant thoughts left my mind. She didn't seem eager to speak to me, and my feet weren't leaping to the floor to speak to her either. This girl, this cousin of mine, this beautiful girl had it going on more than some models. Her skin was white. I was always a pretty good judge of character, and I didn't wanna think she was stuck up, but it was just the way she carried herself. It wasn't with confidence, but with arrogance. That absolutely made me detest her sometimes.

Actually, I forgot why I was mad at her. I didn't remember the incident that caused so much tension between us. Why did we have a wall built between blood relatives? When we were in the sixth and fifth grade—I was in the sixth; she was in the fifth—we used to talk all the time.

Then we spent some time together. Pillar and I came to Grandma's house—the same house I'd last seen her. Something that weekend caused her to not want to be my friend. Something in that time made her not ever want to open up to me. I was sad then, but I am older now and I have the "I don't care" attitude. It had been years, maybe six, since we had last seen one another.

There she stood before me. Should I continue being dumb, not saying anything, or should I break the wall? Pillar went off on me one time, our last time together many years ago. Maybe that was why I didn't want to communicate.

As I thought of my grandfather clinging to life, I realized he wouldn't be pleased with this strife between his granddaughters. And although I didn't know how to make it better, I knew I could at least try. If she went off on me again, then it would be on her.

As Pillar saw me walking towards her, her blank stare turned into a slight smile. I kept looking over my shoulder because I knew she couldn't be smiling at me with all this distance that's been between us. Luckily I was wrong.

When I got closer, she uttered, "Hello Payton. I see you're all grown up. Six years have changed both of us, huh? We're not kids anymore. How ya doin'? You're *so* quiet. Give me a hug."

I was so quiet because I was overwhelmed. It was natural for me to assume that she was putting on airs. After all, there were several others in the house, including my mom, who loved this girl, and she would never let them see the ugly side of her. But, I felt the sincerity in her approach.

I wanted to get to know this person more. This time I wanted to rekindle our childhood. I wanted my cousin back as my friend.

Growing up is never easy, but although life courses changed, God stayed constant. Just as I climbed over the barrier and started to mend my relationship with Pillar, I hoped all of the other things in life that had me horrified could be overcome in Christ. God seems to make the scary things not so scary, and if I get up the nerve and stay in

God's will, I can conquer anything and be scared of nothing.

After that point, I wasn't scared about the possibility of losing my grandfather. God knows what He's doing at all times. By giving my worries to Him, I no longer have to be burdened down. Finally even in my turmoil, I was renewed. I was ready to start facing my fears.

Agreeing to Disagree

"*W*hat've you done to your hair?" my cousin, Pillar, said to me at my grandparents' home.

I had tiny spiral curls in my hair, "the twists." some people called them. I thought they were kinda cute. At that point they were kinda frizzy because of the rain the past weekend, but surely I didn't think it looked bad.

"It's just a style the hairdresser did," I said, trying not to have a confrontation.

Pillar gave her unsolicited opinion. "Girl, you need to wash that out. It looks . . . worn . . . not fresh."

The phone rang at the house. Luckily that prevented me from tellin my "cuz" a few things. Everyone was at the edge of their seats, hoping for good news. My father answered the phone.

After a minute of dialogue, Dad yelled, "He's gonna be all right. Dad's OK! He's gonna pull through."

Pillar instantly hugged me. I needed that embrace. Though her sass and brash demeanor irked me, the hug let me get past that.

We all screamed. It was truly exciting. My cousin and I, remarkably, had been getting along. It was actually quite scary because I had always been timid around her. Timid because her outer beauty was so phenomenal to me. I always felt insecure around her. Like I didn't measure up. This time maybe I had been through so much this past year that trivial things like appearance were no longer barriers for me, or maybe it was that Pillar had grown herself, because she seemed to appreciate who I was. I so liked the new relationship that was developing with my cousin.

Mom immediately picked up on the vibes between us, and she went out on a limb and invited Pillar down to spend a couple of weeks this summer. Now, normally this would've been too much for me to handle. My cousin and I hadn't even seen each other in years, much less spent time with one another for a week or two, but if today was any indication of what could be, I was ready to spend time with my flesh and blood. Hopefully our future could be filled with great memories.

Since my grandfather was doing better, my father was the only one in my immediate family that was staying a couple of days. Mom decided that Perry and I needed to make school the next day, so she drove us home. Sitting in the backseat of the car, I decided I needed to talk to Tad. So I called him up on my cell phone to see if he could meet me up at my home.

"Hey, baby," I told him, forgetting my mom was in the front seat.

"What'd you say?" she cut in to my conversation.

Without responding to my mother, I quickly changed my tone of voice. "Um, what are you doing? You think you could come over tonight?"

Tad replied, "I'm a little tired. Let's get together tomorrow, 'cause I do need to see you."

"Ohhh, please come. I need my spirits lifted badly."

"I know you aren't begging someone to come over," Mom scolded.

"No, no Mom," I replied back. "Tad, I really need to talk to you if we can. Can you just come over for a while," I whispered softly in the phone so that my mom wouldn't hear me. I hated that she was listening. Surely she hated the way her refined daughter was talking on the phone. Inside I knew I needed to not be so forward.

"That's cool," he said. "Since you insist . . . I'll come."

After I hung up the phone, I leaned to the front of the car. My mother and I had some issues to discuss, one being when we were going to look for my new prom dress. The second was how late my curfew was going to be. Since my prom was only a week away, I knew I had to address the subject. I would have preferred to have done it with my brother, Perry, not in the car. He can sometimes be annoying and mess up what I'm trying to have happen. However, I didn't have time for strategy and planning. I just had to attack and hope that my mom would go for what I wanted.

"Hey Ma . . . about my prom dress. Ahhh . . . when are we going shopping?"

"I beg your pardon, Payton Skky?"

A lump went in my throat. Just then I knew it wasn't going to be as easy as I thought it was going to be to accomplish my task.

"Ma, I—I need a dress."

"What do you mean you need a dress? I just bought you a beautiful fuscia gown that you wore not too long ago. Now, was that to your school?"

"No ma'am."

"Then what's the problem?" she asked innocently.

I rationalized, "I wore it. I wore it out. I wore it with Tad, and he's taking me to my prom. Surely I don't want him to see me in the same dress."

"Well, since you surely don't have a job, I think you better get used to the fact that you're going to be wearing that same beautiful fuscia gown. It looks lovely on you."

I leaned back in the car and hit my head on the backseat. I was angry. I never really wanted to work, but this was one of those times when I wished I still worked at my dad's dealership. Feeling defeated, I didn't even address the other issue, feeling it was a lost cause, but something inside me said, hey, all she could say was no, which she'd already said before, so what could I lose? Feeling I could only gain, I tried.

"Hey Mom, what about curfew prom night? You know we talked about me staying out all night last year?"

"Well, I've thought about that, and I know it's a special night for you. What I've decided is for you to have an after-prom breakfast."

"What's that?" my brother said as if he read my mind.

"After prom you have a small group of friends over, eat breakfast, and dialogue around a beautifully decorated dining room table. All guests have permission from their parents, and yes, I'm around, but I'm not in the room, and it's over at about 5 AM. So basically, you're up all night, Payton. How does that sit for curfew?"

Although she was trying to trick me, it sounded pretty good. My friends coming over to my house for breakfast. I liked it. Yeah, I liked it a lot.

"That sounds great, Mom," I said to her.

"Well, you better get to planning, because I need to hear from everybody's parents before they come over."

"Yes ma'am."

In my mind, I started planning my guest list.

"And it doesn't need to be a ton of people, so don't start inviting the whole school. It's an intimate breakfast party. The smaller the number, the better."

"Hey baby," I said to Tad as I hugged him later that evening. "Oh, it's so good to see you. I missed you so much. Well, I might as well get ready and prepare you; my mom's not buying me another prom dress. I'm so mad because I'll be in the same thing that you've already seen me in, but—"

"Payton," Tad interrupted.

I was hogging the conversation, and he wanted to cut in. I didn't even realize he was trying to cut me off, but after I heard him call my name, I looked over at him.

"Yes?"

"That's what I wanted to talk to you about. I won't be able to take you to your prom."

No way! Surely he didn't say what I thought he said. No way!

"What do you mean? Please explain, because obviously I'm not hearing you right. I thought I heard you say you wouldn't be able to take me to my prom. Please tell me that's not what I heard."

Reluctantly, he said, "You heard right."

"Why?" I questioned, absolutely upset.

"I know you're upset, but really you shouldn't be. I mean, we did just go to my prom."

"Yeah, we went to your prom. But what about my prom? You went to your school with your friends, and I went there with you. I put everything off and made sure I was with you. You didn't even dance with me or pay attention to me, until you saw someone else dance with me, but I knew you were busy. Now you can't even accompany me to mine. That's foul. I wanna know what's so important that you can't change it."

"I made a commitment to go to an FCA camp long before I realized the date of your prom. It's my mistake, obviously poor planning, but I didn't even realize the dates were the same time. And I'm a huddle leader. This ministry has given me so much over the last four years. Now it's time for me to give something back. And I have to go because I can't get out of it."

There were no words that I could have used to tell him how I felt. OK, so he wanted to go to a Christian conference. That was sweet, but he was my guy, and surely he shouldn't go. My prom was more important than that, but he didn't see it that way, and it really hurt.

"Well, what do you expect me to do? Since you're saying you're not going to get out of it."

"Well, like I said, we already went to a prom. I expect you to stay home and just kinda . . . get over it."

"Get over it?!"

"Well maybe I shouldn't have said get over it. That was pretty harsh."

"Yeah, you're right; that was pretty harsh," I said to him with an attitude.

"If you don't want to stay home, go alone. That's how most people at my school do it."

"This isn't your school." I voiced with even more attitude, "You know what? I don't even want to talk about this now, Tad, because obviously you don't see it the way I do. And I don't wanna say something that would just not be good for our relationship, because I can't believe you can't put off *whatever* to go with me."

"I can't believe you don't think doing something for God is a lot more important than taking you out dancing."

"Good night," came from my lips as I walked over to the front door of my home and opened it. "I don't want you to think I'm being a baby, or a brat, or spoiled, but I don't agree with what you're saying, and I'm angry."

"Well, sleep on it. I'm glad your grandfather is doing well. I missed you and, um, we'll talk later in the week."

He reached over to kiss my hand and I snatched it away from his mouth. I didn't need him to pacify me. Unless he was willing to change his mind and go with me to my prom, he was gon' deal with one hot sister.

Driving to school with Rain, I told her the whole story. She was totally in line with what I was saying. She, too, couldn't believe that my guy couldn't put off his plans to be with me on my special senior night.

"Girl, I can't believe that. You know he wrong."

"I know! That's what I'm screamin'," I told her. "Of course my smart, lil' perfect Tad doesn't see it that way. *I'm* being selfish. Whatever. Hmph, I'm definitely not stayin' home on prom night, and I'm surely not going by myself. Only problem is . . . everybody already has a date."

"Well, maybe not everybody," Rain said.

"What do you mean?"

"Last I heard, Mr. Dakari—"

"Well, first of all, I don't know if he'd even want to take me, and second, even if he wanted to take me, I don't know if I'd want him to."

"Let's take one thing at a time," my friend Rain said. "You know I can't have you alone on prom night. The crew is talking about getting an RV or something."

"An RV? Ya'll don't wanna get a car from my dad's place?" I questioned, a tad offended.

"Nah, we did that last year. We want to hang out. Park out in the parking lot and have a party or something. I don't know, do something crazy. You know Mr. Skky wants the cars back on the lot as soon as we leave the facility. You can't do that by yourself. Plus, you know you ain't never got over Dakari."

"Yeah, right," I told her. "I'm in love with somebody that's not Dakari. I don't know. The whole idea is crazy. Forget it."

I had waited to be a senior my whole life, and it was finally here. Unfortunately, my senior year was passing so quickly before my eyes. As I sat in sixth period I had nothing to do because new cheerleaders were already in place. I pulled out my pad and started writing down the people I wanted to invite to my breakfast. My list was so extensive. Everyone had a date but me. Then I remembered what my mom said. Checking out the list, I wondered if I wanted all these people over to my house. Fifty people, well, forty-nine—I kept forgetting I didn't have a date. Nope. *Too many,* I thought while I balled up the paper and threw it in the trash.

"What was that?" my old buddy Dakari said as he sat down beside me on the bleachers. "You just threw my love letter away! I wanted to read it."

"Ha ha! Quit joking. You're such a trip," I teased back at him.

"I like that outfit, lady. You know you look pretty as always. It's been a while since we've talked. What's been up?"

"It hasn't been that long. I saw you that night of Lynzi's accident. I thank you again for being there for me. It was hard. You're really a good friend, you know that?"

"Well, I care," he said sincerely. "I care about you. So, um, I've been talking to your friend, Rain."

I braced myself for what was about to come. Although I told Rain to drop it, I knew somehow she wouldn't. Here it was about to come. Either I needed to brace myself for being let down easy or I would have to decide whether or not I was going to accept an invitation from my ex-boyfriend to go to our senior prom.

"I never thought I'd have an opportunity to ask you to go with me to the prom since I messed up earlier in the year. Remember when we were sophomores and we wanted to go to the prom? Last year we hoped to be King and Queen. I just can't forget. And after talkin' to your friends, I now know that yo' boy won't be able to take you. And since I'm all alone . . . "

"What do you mean 'all alone'? I thought you and Starr—"

"Now c'mon. You know we are not together. She's probably taking one of her college boys or something. Would you go to the prom with me?" he asked softly as he leaned towards my face.

Without thinking, I responded, "I'd love to."

I didn't answer from the present. I answered from the past. He was right. This guy had been my whole high school life. He was a big part of my time at Lucy Laney. It only seemed fitting to go to my senior prom with him. What did Tad have to do with it anyway? I asked myself in absolute denial.

Two days later, I was at my home studying for a test, and someone blew the horn. No one was at home but me. So when I went outside, I saw Tad standing outside with a bunch of roses. They were beautiful. But I was still angry, and roses were not going to make me forgive him. So, I didn't take them.

He went on to say, "I'm sorry you don't understand. I love you so much and I would never want to hurt you or let you down. I just made a commitment to the Lord, and I think He has something for me in going to this conference. If I don't go, I won't get what He has prepared for me there. I wish you were at a place where you understood. But I've been praying for it to be OK with you, and I know that He will show you that I'm not trying to be unsupportive for your thing. But at this time, I'm called to do His thing."

"Well, I hear you, and I'm not saying that doing something for God is not important, but I really can't believe that you're not supposed to take me to my prom. You know what? It's working out though. Don't even worry about me."

"What do you mean, 'it's working out'? You're going to it?"

"Yeah, I'm going," I said to him boldly.

"Well, I think that's great. Being by yourself, I'm sure they'll be plenty of people who'll dance with you, and you'll be able to hang out with your girls."

"Well, they'll have dates, Tad. They all have dates."

I couldn't bring myself to tell him that I would too. So I didn't. Not that I needed his permission, but surely he deserved to know. I couldn't say it. I led him to believe that I was going alone.

"I'm sorry. I still sense this anger in your voice," Tad spoke with compassion

"Yeah, anger's there. I'll admit. But you know, like I said, don't even worry about it. You just get in your car and go on back home to South Carolina. Get your bags packed for your little camping trip, and let's just not worry about me at my little 'ole prom. I don't understand your decision, and I'm definitely not supporting it. You do what you have to do, and I'll do what I gotta do. So let's just say on this issue we're agreeing to disagree."

13

Hiding
the Truth

*H*e doesn't understand you the way I do," Dakari told me in the Winnebago the night of our prom.

It was weird. I felt prettier in this dress than I did the night I was with Tad. Yet, everything about this night was not exactly on the up and up. When the Winnebago pulled up to my house, my girlfriends came to get me. I think my parents just sort of assumed I was going alone as well, since Tad wasn't accompanying me. Dakari wasn't part of that equation. I didn't really think I was lying; I just sort of thought I was keeping some of the facts to myself.

Dakari had always been a cutie, but that night, in his sweet, black tux, he looked like a dream. The way I was checkin' him out told me there were some feelings inside that weren't resolved when it came to him. And that wasn't a good thing. I missed him. Yeah, the way I stared him up and down, I missed him. It wasn't that I wanted him or needed him; it was that I missed him. It was comforting for at least one night to be by his side.

"Heeeyyyy! Party over here! Party over here! Party over here! Party in here!" we all started chanting as we drove to the prom.

It was such a blast. Lynzi, although she'd missed school, managed to get remarkably better and be up in the place in her red tea-length gown. Dymond looked so pretty in her short cream-colored dress. Rain's long, pink gown was beautiful. She looked like a model straight out of any magazine.

"It's the whole crew again," Lynzi shouted. "Look at us. Well, OK Tyson, you ain't a part of our school, but you know we claim you."

For three years all of us had hung out together. Lynzi was right, and Tad never felt totally comfortable with all of us. Even when he was around, I was a bit on edge. Feeling that my friends didn't measure up to what and who they needed to be. Although they weren't where they needed to be in Christ, we sure had a bond. And as we drove to the prom, that special bond seemed to be unbreakable.

"This Winnebago thing is cool," Fatz blabbed from the driver's seat.

"You just hold it steady, big boy," Dakari told him as he went up front and patted him on the back.

"I got you, man. I got you. We gon' get there in one piece," Fatz said as he came to an abrupt stop at the traffic light and we all braced ourselves.

"All right now," Bam said. "Don't make me hafta pull out one of these brews to calm you down."

Brew, I thought to myself. *What's up? I didn't bargain for this.* I got up and looked in the refrigerator and was dumbfounded by what I saw. The whole refrigerator was packed with beer bottles. I knew Bam was behind it. Oh, I detested Lynzi going out with him.

"People! I wanna know what's up wit' this? This is not even hardly cool. What's up? I thought we agreed no alcohol!"

115

"We agreed not to drink alcohol at the prom," Bam said. "We didn't agree not to have none in the ride."

How did I get myself in this mess? I thought.

"If one of ya'll drink this—I mean any one of these cans, I'm not riding in this car."

"I'm with her," Rain said.

I petitioned, "All ya'll need to be with me. Haven't we had enough experiences of how this can't be good? Hello? I'm serious."

The guys started laughing as if to pass off what I said. They agreed, but not really. I had had it.

I went up to Dakari and said, "I'm serious. I'm not traveling in the car with ya'll drinking. Now if it starts, I'm outta here."

"Calm down, precious," he said as he pulled one of my Shirley Temple curls.

That gesture made my mind switch from being frustrated to being a bit mesmerized. What was happening? I had no clue.

Lord, I thought as I sat at the table riding to my prom, *I feel sort of bad coming to You knowing that I have been deceitful, but I think I might be a little in over my head. Help me.*

When the Winnebago parked, we all got excited. We were at our senior prom. "Going in Style to Bigger Things" was the theme of our prom. So the idea of coming in a big 'ole Winnebago was pretty cool. All our classmates stopped and turned to see who exited. One would've thought we were famous or something. It was cool.

Our crew had always been known as "The Stuff", and the fact of us all being together made eyes turn. We had Dymond, the coolest girl in the projects and the valedictorian of our class. We had Tyson, who didn't even go to our school, but was one of the hottest guys in town, being the star of our rival school. Then there was Bam, the class clown. Everybody loved him because he was too crazy and wild. Dakari, every girl's dream, at our school anyway. Then Lynzi, Rain, and myself. Those people folks always called, you know, "Those Girls." Though I never asked for this image, people always kind of wanted to be us, wanted to be with us, or wanted to see us.

So when we stepped off in our entourage, lots of people took pictures of us. Some folks I went to school with for four years and didn't even know, knew me. I was glad that I was as popular as I was in school.

We immediately went to take pictures. I was having a ball. There was a table dead in the center that no one had occupied. It was as if they were saving it for us. We had the royal treatment at this prom.

Things were going well until someone else entered the room. It was Starr. She had on a tight black gown that looked fabulous. I couldn't take the props away from the sister. She had it going on. Her long black hair was flowing down the gown, and all the guys were on her, but when her date, a guy named Zeke Pryor, who we found out later was a senior at Morehouse College, walked in, all the ladies' eyes were on him. The brother had it together. He was quite poised. My date seemed to be getting a little rough under the collar when he saw that.

"What's up?" I teased him. "You jealous?"

"Don't even go there. I dropped that chick."

I laughed, "Yeah, OK. Whatever."

"You trippin'," he argued back. "They ain't even fazin' me. Let's dance."

Dakari had always been an assertive young man. He got up, grabbed my arm, and almost tugged me onto the dance floor. I didn't even get to say, "No, I don't wanna dance; I'm tired!" Before I knew it, we were whirling around in front of everyone. And it wasn't even a song I liked. However, when he started talking to me, I was once again under his spell.

"I see in those Bambi eyes that you still feel something

for me," he whispered.

"You're dreaming."

"Am I," he questioned. "I'm not saying I know what's there. I'm not even saying that I believe it's as strong as it used to be. I'm saying there's something still there. You still feel it. This embrace still feels right to both of us."

I was blushing, and although you couldn't tell it because of my brown skin, inside I knew I was blushing. He had me. He called me out. He read me right, and I didn't like it.

I dashed from the floor and went out into the hallway. When I got outside the civic center, the same place where the Debutante Ball had been, my mind raced back to the night I was Tad's date instead of Dakari's. *What was I doing?* I thought. *What was going on with me? Why was I causing problems for myself?*

"I'm right, aren't I?" I heard Dakari say from behind. "You still care."

As I practically ruined my mascara, I said, "So what if I do? It doesn't really matter. Regardless of what I feel for you, I am in love with someone else."

Although we had never been physically linked together, the emotional tie was still tight. I don't think I'd ever even told Tad that something in me still liked Dakari. As the tears trickled down, before I could speak, I felt his lips on my neck.

"No," I said to him. "No."

"There you are," Lynzi said to Dakari and I as she interrupted our very awkward moment. "You guys just won King and Queen of the prom. C'mon."

"Speech! Speech! Speech! Speech! Speech" was chanted from the crowd as the two of us stood on stage.

With the foil crown on my head, I said, "I'll never forget this year. I'll never forget you guys. I'll never forget this school. I'll never forget this moment. Although I'm not close to everyone here, each of you have a place in my heart. I say that because sometimes I hid under the facade of cheerleader or—"

"Rich girl," somebody yelled from the crowd.

"No, I was thinking homecoming queen. And maybe I didn't let myself get as close to you as I possibly could have. Maybe I wasn't as open. Maybe I protected myself. And for that . . . it's my loss. But by giving me this honor, it shows that you cared for me anyway, besides my sometimes ugly ways. For that I'm forever thankful. As we move from this place to bigger and better things, I pray that each of you come to our ten-year reunion with all your dreams accomplished. We're forever one as a class. God Bless," I turned and humbly handed the mike to Dakari.

Working the crowd, he said, "Well, I won't be as serious," and they all started laughing. "And I can't be as beautiful as your Prom Queen, but I do say thank you, and before you all, I confess that I wasn't as much a gentleman to our Prom Queen as I should've been. But standing before her now, I wanna say I'm glad she's my date, and I'm glad she's possibly giving me another chance—"

"Yeahhh," someone echoed again from the crowd that was beginning to annoy me because that was far from the truth.

"And I just wanna show her, in front of all ya'll, how much I really care."

Without any warning, he planted a kiss on my lips. When we were done with the kiss, it was as if something turned my head towards the back door. I hoped my eyes were failing me, because I saw Tad Taylor standing there in a tux! When I blinked he was gone. I might as well have been at one of my earlier years' track meets, as fast as I ran through the crowd. Out the door I flew to find him, to explain, to say something. He was nowhere in sight. Had I just imagined it? Was my conscience getting the best of me? I didn't know.

The guys kept their word, because I never saw them drinking any beer. However, when I opened the refrigerator, as the Winnebago pulled up to my home, I noticed several bottles missing.

"I'm hungry," Fatz said. "Ya'll get out. Let's eat."

My mom had a place elegantly set. Sparkling grape juice, steak, eggs, and pancakes were all a part of the menu. It was a feast for a king and queen, and she was excited that Dakari and I had won that honor at prom night. Caught up in the emotion, it took her a moment to pull me aside and tell me that I had had a visitor earlier in the evening.

"Where's Tad?" Mom questioned.

"What do you mean 'where's Tad'? Remember, he had an FCA something or another to go to. He's out of town."

"No, sweetie. He came over tonight in a tuxedo. He had a corsage in his hand for you and said he wanted to know where the prom was to surprise you, because he came back early."

I could've fainted. I couldn't believe what I was hearing from my mom. Unfortunately, it made sense. I wasn't dreaming. It was Tad earlier. What had I done? Not telling him backfired on me.

I had no clue if anything could be salvaged. I pleaded to go to Tad's home, but my mom wouldn't let me. First of all, it was two in the morning; second, I had a house full of company.

Throughout the night, my mind wasn't in it. Dakari didn't look so cute anymore. The food didn't smell so good. My friends' laughter wasn't consuming me, and I wasn't as proud of my night's accomplishments as I had been earlier. I did, however, try calling Tad's home. The phone was busy.

I figured he was so fed up with me that he'd taken the phone off the hook. I couldn't blame him. I couldn't blame him at all.

Tad loved him some breakfast biscuits from Hardee's. So the next morning, since I was up 'til five, I didn't go to bed. I went by the fast food restaurant and picked him up two sausage biscuits with cheese.

I drove the twenty miles to his place and tapped on his window. It was bad to get him up this early in the morning, but I surely didn't want to ring the doorbell and wake up the whole house. I had to see him. I had to talk to him. I had to see if he was angry. This whole time I was kidding myself, for I knew he was as angry as a grizzly bear wanting food.

Obviously, I tapped on the wrong window, because his mom said, "Payton, honey, is that you?"

I was embarrassed to no end, but that's what I get for trying to be slick. Sooner or later I would learn nothing beats integrity.

"Yes, Mrs. Taylor. I'm so sorry to bother you so early in the morning, but—"

"Say no more, dear; I'll tell Tad you obviously need to see him."

I was pacing back and forth around my Jeep, not knowing what to say, how to start the conversation, or what I would do when I saw him. Suddenly, he appeared before me. His words were correct and saddening.

"Yes, I was there last night. Yes, I saw you get a kiss from your king. Yes, it hurt me. And yes, I have serious questions on where we stand. I don't appreciate you lying, and a lot of this wouldn't have happened if you hadn't been hiding the truth."

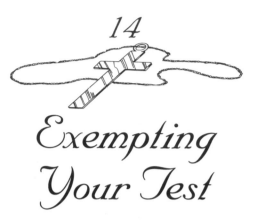

14

Exempting Your Test

I feel drunk," I said to Shayna Mullen, after deciding to sit down with her for some type of spiritual counseling. "I don't know what's wrong with me. I haven't taken a sip of alcohol, but I feel kinda out of it. I mean, if I'm such a Christian, why I do some of the things that I do? Why do I stress out over stuff that's stressing me out?"

She told me that it was neat being in the place where I was because growth could take place. Actually, it didn't feel neat. It was quite confusing. Being honest with myself, I knew I still did like Dakari, but I didn't know why. Supposedly I was so infatuated and totally happy with Tad. So I decided to figure this whole Dakari situation out. Why was he interested in me? Why was he pulling on me in ways that were tugging me to him?

He had invited me over to his place. His parents had cooked dinner for his big brother Drake and Drake's girlfriend, Haley. They had just graduated from the University of Georgia, the place where I'd be entering in the fall. Haley was so cool. Just an opportunity to get a chance to talk to her again would be well worth going over to the Graham's home.

Drake and Haley were an adorable couple. He was absolutely gorgeous, and she was so very beautiful. Now they had graduated and he had a job. I couldn't believe I was sitting in front of a professional football player. A second rounder! He hadn't actually played in the big league, but he had a contract with the Atlanta Falcons. How cool!

As I watched Dakari look at his big brother, he still hadn't gotten over the awe factor. I hoped Dakari would be in that same league, because he wanted it for himself. I don't know what he'd do if he weren't able to be up there with his brother, but it was surely going to be interesting. However, Dakari wouldn't have it easy, being that Tad was slated to be Georgia's top back.

When I noticed Mrs. Graham in the kitchen slaving away, I got up and peeped my head in to see if I could help.

"Sure, baby, c'mon in. You're so sweet," she said to me. "So my son has finally got his senses back. He's trying to date you again, huh?"

I laughed. I loved that she was always in my corner. When Dakari broke up with me in the beginning of the year, she was surely one of my supporters. I wished he would've listened to her then.

"Girl, I wish he would've listened to me a long time ago. Then ya'll could be enjoying ya'll senior year in high school like Drake and Haley enjoyed their senior year at Georgia. But that's all right; you all are going to Georgia too. It just seems so funny. I'm expecting big things, not necessarily out of the relationship. I'm not trying to put any pressure there, but I'm expecting big things from you in school, young lady. And even where my son is concerned . . . You keep your head in them books. You're a smart girl, and I don't want anything spoiling it, especially not the tack-head jokers."

That's why I always liked her. She always put my needs above supporting me following behind her son. That was really something. That showed that she cared about me.

I reached over to give her a big hug and said, "You know, I missed you. Happy early Mother's Day."

Mother's Day was in a couple of days; I figured, why not start celebrating it with someone who deserved well wishes? Mrs. Graham was together. Though we hadn't been in touch lately, she was up-to-date on all my accomplishments.

Mrs. Graham had laid out dinner—or actually, I should say feast—from one table to another. Her husband and her boys were not being skimpy on the choosing. They were eating some of everything.

"My sons are so lucky. Look at these beautiful girls they got at this table. Umh, umh, umh, but if ya'll gonna be with them for a while, I sure hope you can cook like the lady I got," Mr. Graham tastelessly joked.

Dakari wasn't even my boyfriend, so I surely didn't want to comment. We were nowhere near walking down the aisle together, so it's really like Mr. Graham's comment went in one ear and out the other.

However, Drake put his arm around Haley and said, "She can throw down, Dad; she can throw down."

"All right then son, that's what I'm talking 'bout."

We all slightly giggled.

Drake got up and went into the kitchen to get dessert with his mom. What a gentleman, I thought. Dakari sat right there and didn't lift a finger to help. However, he was so cute. I was really getting confused now. He kept looking at me and smiling as if he was so happy I was there. Yet, I kept remembering what Mrs. Mullen told me in our session.

I need to stay focused on Christ. Not guys. Christ.

I was pulled out of that thought when a piece of apple cobbler—homemade apple cobbler, that is—was placed in front of me. Boy, did it look good. Everyone started eating, and Drake kept talking. It was really cute though, because he was talking about how much he loved his Haley.

"Being at Georgia has been such a great experience. Not necessarily because of what I've done with football, and not even being able to graduate on time, which is always a challenge for us football players. But it's with all the cool friends I've made, and 'cause that's where I met my lady."

I looked up at Haley and she had a mouthful of food. I could tell she wanted to smile, but it seemed as if something was stuck in her teeth. She was being so polite that she didn't want to make a big deal of it, but I could tell she needed to spit it out before she choked. She reached for her napkin, finally, and put it up to her face.

When she pulled it away, Drake said, "And I hope that diamond in your mouth tastes good, but I'm sure it would look even better on your finger." He got down on one knee and said, "Will you marry me? I know you've got to get your master's and several other things you want in life. I also know you are planning to go back to Georgia and finish. Your classes are only two days a week, so why not commute from Atlanta? Be my bride. I love you."

Dipping the ring in the water, I noticed a tear trickling down not only Haley's face, but Mrs. Graham's and mine as well. It was so sweet. Such a special moment.

Dakari, my friend, noticing my emotions, grabbed my hand and said, "I'm so glad you're here."

I could only smile back at him. It was too meaningful to miss. I was glad I was there, too. No other place I'd rather be at that moment, for that time.

It was so neat to hear Haley say, "Yes! Yes, I'd love to marry you. You jerk, I'd love to marry you. You tricked me this whole time," she said taking her fist and jamming it into his stomach. "But my parents . . . I gotta ask . . . "

The telephone rang. I looked at the clock; it was exactly 6 P.M., and it was Haley's parents saying congratulations. I hated that they couldn't be there, but later I found out that they were up in Maryland visiting Haley's sick grandmother.

Lord, I thought as I was in the bathroom washing my hands, *this is hard. Help me see who's just kinda supposed to be my guy, or friend. Maybe I don't need a boyfriend? But that's not what I'm sensing, because my feelings for Dakari are growing with this experience, not diminishing, which I hoped they would. I just kinda felt they would. Help me clarify things, please.*

When I opened the door, I saw Drake and Dakari in the hallway. It just seemed too uncomfortable to just walk between them. I knew they were enjoying their moment. So I stepped back in and closed the door. I figured I needed more time to think anyway. Yet their voices grew louder, and once again I was in a place of hearing them discuss me, and their topic disgusted me.

Dakari said boastfully, "So, um, give me my money, man. I won the bet."

"What you mean you won the bet? You done got with dat?"

"Naw, man. I kissed her though, at the prom."

"Kissed? Tuh! Naw, my brother. It ain't even all about that. Don't even try to cop out. All the way, or no way. You know the deal."

"All the way, or no way," I mouthed to the mirror. Are you kidding me? This is crazy. Why is this always discussed? Same stuff that happened in the beginning of the year. I'm sick of this. I had pumped myself up so much in the bathroom that I immediately walked out, stepped up to Dakari, and forcefully spoke. The head was movin'. The

126

eyes were rollin'. And the finger was swayin'.

"So this is what this is all about. This is why you've been so nice to me, to win a stupid bet with your brother. Oh my gosh."

I looked at Drake and said, "I thought you were so cool. I thought you were all that and you are such a chump, pushing him up to something like that. Respect is gone."

I walked away. Dakari tried to grab my arm. I jerked it from him.

"Don't even try it. Don't even think about it. You're a trip. Your foul tactics were working. I was really falling for you. How stupid am I? Well, dumb no more. Bye!"

I went into the dining room and thanked Mrs. Graham again for such a wonderful evening. I was trying to hold back the emotion, because I was really feeling dirty. I couldn't even tell Haley congratulations. I was so angry at Drake, I didn't know if she was getting a good catch or not. One thing I was not, was a fake person. So, I merely smiled at her.

"We'll talk soon," I told her as I exited the place.

Dakari had left me with no option. It had proved to be a no-brainer. Tad was the one for me. There again, why would I ever doubt that? Why would I ever question that? Why would I ever want it to be someone else, when I had a guy who was so pure in the heart? Whose sole mission was to please God. Whom I could now see cared more about pleasing Him than pleasing me, and yet, that still wasn't enough for me. That still wasn't good; I still thought I should've been first, and even in that whole thing, dropping his plans to come surprise me, how special. Yet, I ruined that moment because I was with someone else.

There was only one thing to say to Tad. Nothing but one thing to do. Nothing could right my wrong. I had to talk to

Tad, and I needed to do it soon. I had tried to call him for two days. It was Monday again, and that was no good. I wanted to talk to him so bad, but I just didn't want to drop over to his house anymore and bang on the window. I think Mrs. Taylor had had enough surprises of that kind from me to last a lifetime, but I had to do something. I needed to talk to him.

My math teacher Mrs. Brinks said, "Payton, congratulations. You don't have to take the exam."

I was the only one in my class who didn't have to take that test, and since my last class that day was cheerleading, it was safe to say I wouldn't have to take one exam. I was glad to see my schoolwork hadn't suffered through all this drama. That was exciting. The bell rung, and another day of my senior year had dwindled away. I was headed to my car, and Dakari stepped in my view.

"I don't want to embarrass you in front of all these folks. But I will. You best get out of my way," I told him.

"We need to talk," Dakari persisted.

"No. You need to get out of my way. If we talk, it'll be when I'm ready. Right now I've said all I have to say. Don't make me get loud 'cause you know a sister can."

He got out of my way, but as I walked several feet from him, he yelled, "I'ma call you, girl. I'ma call you tonight."

I didn't worry about speaking to him. *My machine will be screening my calls,* I thought.

I hated just going over to Tad's school, but I needed to talk to him. *I'll do it one more time,* I thought. I headed over to Silver Bluff. I didn't want to get embarrassed by the principal again, so I waited right beside Tad's car. He had to come out some time. I just hoped some time would be soon. It took him no time to exit out the building this time, but he was with that girl. It was uncomfortable, but I knew I couldn't be angry. He had seen someone kiss me. At least he was only walking with this girl. Deep down, I knew her motives were probably just as devious as Dakari's. I couldn't get mad at him.

When he saw my car beside his, I didn't want to be embarrassed. Therefore, I didn't get out. I sat there to see what he'd do. If he kept talking to her, then I'd just collect myself and drive away. He didn't. I was glad he didn't. He said something to her and she left. He came over to my car, and I let down the window.

"I'd like to talk to you if I could. I don't know how much time I got. You don't have to explain anything. It won't take much time. Do you wanna get in?"

He came around the passenger's side and got into my Jeep.

"You know, I'll cut right to it," I said to him. "I've been a jerk. I wanted more from you. I wanted to be more to you than God. I didn't think you cared enough for me, and sometimes I don't know what I was thinking, but, um, I know I love you. But . . . you don't deserve my shabby love. You deserve much more. You were kind not to break up with me when I know that's what you wanted to do. Maybe I should do it. I'm the one that has to do it. I'm the one that has to set you free. It's like you're a dove and I'm clipping your wings. I'm trying to get better, but you deserve better. You deserve someone who's trying to attain a high level of maturity, in their Christian walk. Hopefully you won't be running into someone's arms like I did, but the girl you were just walking with—"

"No," he cut me off and said. "We just found out we have to take the physics test next week. The only test I gotta take is physics. I've never been as smart as you, but anyway, she's gonna help me, so we're gonna study together."

"You don't owe me an explanation."

"I know, I just wanted to give you one," he said.

"I don't have to take any of my tests."

"Well, you've earned it. You worked hard, studied hard.

You should be rewarded in that way."

"And that's why I've gotta let you go, Tad," I said as I became really upset. "You worked hard on being a great boyfriend to me. You gave me everything I could ever want in a relationship. You were there. You cared. I failed miserably in assessing what was going on between us. And now I know I truly have to let you go. I took you through so much, and you didn't deserve that. Just like we got rewarded in our classes, so too did you deserve to be exempting your test."

15

Walking with Grace

I had walked away from him when I said it was over. I guess it was 'cause I couldn't look him in the face. Couldn't allow him to see my pain. Couldn't let him know I wanted our relationship to continue.

He came up behind me and placed his arms around my waist and uttered, "I've been trying to get you out of my mind the past couple of days. Yeah, I was extremely angry and disturbed by what I saw . . . my girl with another guy. But I couldn't shake Payton Skky. I'm in love with you, and I want to work through all the bad stuff. I don't wanna just throw in the towel. Relationships take work; that's why I want us to take it easy and keep it before God, so that stuff like this doesn't happen. But we're human. We're gonna hurt each other. We're gonna make mistakes. Maybe if we try the approach of being best friends, the need to stray won't come up. Whatever we decide, I don't wanna hear talk of us not being together."

I turned around and hugged him. I grabbed his neck so

tight, he probably thought I was trying to choke him. I had received yet another blessing. One I surely didn't deserve, but I was going to be gracious and accept it anyway and try to deserve it.

When I got home that day, my three girlfriends were plastered over my bed. Seeing them was unexpected. However, I was happy to see them and the 'Thank You' balloons they brought.

"What's up with this?" I said to them.

All three of them came up to me and gave me a hug.

"We love you, Girrrl. We understand that it's so hard being our friend," Dymond said.

I shook my head and joked, "Yeah."

She said, "No, seriously. You got us out of some tight stuff this year, and we just wanted to say that we do appreciate it, and we're gonna spend some time growing in the Word. Not to say that we're gonna be where you are—"

"I'm not even where I'm supposed to be," I cut her off and said.

Dy continued, "Yeah, well, you're further than we are. And about the incident that I had early this year . . . you know, smokin' that stuff. I . . . I don't even know how I got there. That wasn't even me. If it hadn't been for you, I don't know how many I would've smoked that night, or if I would've done it again another day. I haven't ever really told you thank you, but it meant the world."

Rain came up to me next and said, "You've been my best friend ever since we were in preschool. Well, now we're about to go our separate ways. At least we'll be in the state of Georgia."

"So we better get together," I told her.

"Yeah, we will. Distance won't keep us apart, right?"

"Right," I told her.

Rain continued, "I just want you to know that I'm still pure, and I owe that in large part to you. I really feel like

God used you to save me in that area. I just need to say, Thanks! What a friend to go against the norm and tell me I was trippin'."

"Don't give me too much credit. I realized I'm not too far from those feelings myself," I told her honestly.

"Yeah, but if you hadn't have told me what I was thinking was wrong, I might've been telling you a month later I regretted doing what I was about to do."

My tall friend leaned down and kissed me on the cheek. Now I was really emotional. It was so good to hear that Rain still was practicing abstinence from sex. Both heaven and I were pleased.

Just looking at Lynzi being alive made a tear fall. She didn't have to say a thing. I was so thankful she was alive. She couldn't even speak.

She crossed her arms across her heart and said, "You know how much you mean to me. You know what you've done for me."

She started to cry and we all hugged her. Then we all hugged each other. I was so blessed. Not to just have Tad, but to have my friends understand where I was trying to take them and for me to understand that I'm not that capable of leading. We all have to be humble daily before our Father to get to a level where He wants us to be.

The next day, I was at a tea with The Links. It was a mother-daughter tea in celebration of all of the Links who had daughters who were graduating, as well as Mother's Day being upon us. My mother took the platform to say a few words at the end of the occasion.

As she made her way to the front, Summer, who was at my table, leaned over and said, "I haven't seen you in the past month or so. How've you been?"

"Good," I told her.

"Aren't you going to Georgia?"

"Yeah."

"Well, hopefully we can hook up up there. I'm going too."

"I thought you were going to some art school, drama school, or some big-time school in New York."

"Um, well, I didn't get in," she said with despair.

This girl had always been confident, beautiful, and outgoing, and the cousin of my rival—who's now, luckily, not my rival—Starr. However, I couldn't believe Summer and I were actually able to have a decent conversation with each other. Things do change when maturity sets in.

"Well, I'll look forward to being with you at Georgia. You're a gymnast; are you going to try out for the team?"

"Yeah, well, actually, I don't have to try out. I got a scholarship."

"That's sooo cool," I told her.

"Yeah, but I'm gonna need some friends. I don't make them as easily as you do."

"Well, you already got one friend. I don't know about making new ones, but we'll look out for each other up there. OK?"

Our conversation was cut off by my mom's authoritative voice.

"Young ladies, we're proud of you. We have nurtured you for years. We have raised you from tots to beautiful young women. We will miss you as you venture out into whatever endeavor God is about to put before your path. We hope that you remember this organization, because we will be praying for you as you go your ways. I want to also thank you for being leaders of our debutantes this year. You all have grown up knowing what is expected of debs, but when young ladies from our surrounding areas join us they aren't as polished. Yet, you ladies carried them with your poise. We thank you for making this year's debutante group and cotillion one of our best yet. You've set the precedent that will be hard for others to follow. However, we look forward to allowing those girls to rise to the same high standard that you did this year. We'll miss you greatly. And to my precious baby, Payton Skky, who has grown into someone who's made me extremely proud, keep growing in you and keep growing in God. When you go to Georgia, I'm just a phone call away. I am your mother, but I'm also your friend. I'm here to help you go through whatever is before you. I love you, and we love you all."

I went up and kissed my mom on the cheek and told her how much I loved her. Everyone stood up and gave us an ovation. It was pretty cool to be shining on stage with my mom, an awesome lady of God.

"Shayna," I said over the phone.

"Yes, this is she."

"Hi, it's Payton."

"Well, how are you?"

"Things are going good. Actually, since we spoke a week ago, I have a better perspective."

"Well, that's exciting. I have a Scripture for you," she told me.

"Oh, cool."

"Got a pen?"

"Yes ma'am."

"It's 2 Peter 1:1–12."

"What's it about?"

"No. You read it and call me back. I know you have graduation coming up, so why don't we plan on getting together the first of June, when all your festivities are over."

"That sounds great. I'll call you. I hope you come to my graduation."

"Well, Memorial Day weekend is my fifth-year anniversary. I don't know where my precious man is taking me, but we're not going to be in town. However, you will be in my thoughts. Believe that, darling, I hope you remember that day, too, make it one of the most special ones of your life. It's a tremendous accomplishment, and I'm really proud of you. We'll talk soon. Bye."

"Bye-bye."

"Thanks, God," I said as I hung up the phone. "Thanks for sending me Shayna. She is awesome. Thanks."

The baccalaureate service for my school was held on Mother's Day, and since I was Student Government Association Vice-President, I decided to have it at my church. My pastor was so eloquent in charging people, both with the gospel and with moving in positive directions. My class needed both, and I was excited he'd agreed to give it to us. Before the service started, I noticed Tad in the hallway.

I went up to him and said, "Hey, guy! Thanks for coming."

He said, "I'm glad to be here. This is big moment for you. Missed one, don't want to miss another"

The smile he gave me melted my soul with warmth. It was as if we were the only two people on Earth. Being that Dakari went to my school, he was there. He found his way to us. I saw him from across the room, and I hoped deep inside that he would keep walking, but he stopped. Just my luck, he stopped.

"Um, I owe you two an apology," he humbled himself and said. "I disrespected both of you, and I'm sorry. Um, Tad man, I never should have kissed yo' girl. I do hope one day she's my girl, but until then, sorry man. And Payton, contrary to what you heard the other day at my home, my motives were right, not wrong. Trying to keep up with my big brother sometimes gets me into trouble, but, um, I didn't mean to hurt you. I'm sorry. It's not too many of US up at Georgia, so um . . . I hope we can put all this behind us and become friends."

The two guys slapped hands.

"It's cool, man," Tad told him, and I simply smiled, holding Tad's hand tightly and not letting go.

Dakari saw the gesture and looked dejected. As he walked away, I was glad he did stop. Sad that it wasn't an "us" anymore. Glad it was an "us" at one time. He was a good guy. He just wasn't the guy for me.

"And so I charge you guys not to forget Christ next year. Not to let people tell you you can't be all that you can be. Because in Him, you can be whatever you want to be. You can be more than you can ever dream of. I charge you seniors to soar high, and I hope that when you stumble, you will remember Christ there, too. Payton? Payton Skky, you asked me to say some words to your class, but I think you got a few things that you need to say to them. So at this time I call you up to the pulpit to speak on what this year has meant to you."

I almost dropped to my knees when I heard my pastor say those words. I didn't have anything to say, anything to share with my parents, my friends, my guy, or my God. What could I say? Yet, I couldn't just sit there and say, "Oh no, Pastor, I don't have anything to say. You called on the wrong sister." So I had to get up and speak from the heart.

"In 2 Peter it says you need to be righteous, holy, and living your life to glorify God. I've learned so much being in high school, and especially this year. Who am I really living my life for, me or Him? I had to ask the tough questions. I've been placed in tough situations, and I can honestly stand here in front of you today, about to graduate from high school, and I still am a little unsure of where my life is

137

going. I guess I learned that I should be unsure, that I shouldn't learn the future, that I shouldn't even know the day I'm going to be with God in heaven. He is in control of my life, and if I surrender everything in my life to Him, I don't have to worry. The trick is not saying it, but living it."

Pausing, I so hoped my words were sinking in. Every person in my class needed to hear this. For in order to make it out in the world, they needed to possess sober faith. Yet, I needed to be real with them. I needed to make sure they got it.

"I understand what it means to be with your boyfriend and want to go a little further than the Lord says you should. I understand what it means to have peer pressure and want to go with the crowd just because. I understand what it means to want to follow friends towards destruction, even if the crowd is going against what God says you should do. I've been there when alcohol is thrown in your face and you just wanna take a sip. We know that's wrong; shoot, we aren't legally able to buy the stuff. But what helps you say no? What helps you stay sober? I learned being able to trust God with my life is being sober. It's being a sober Christian. It's fasting, praying, and being in His Word. It's loving my neighbor as myself. It's being in church, it's going to Sunday school, it's using my gifts for Him, and it's love. If you're not practicing those things, you're a drunk Christian. I mean, you are not at your full capacity when it comes to spiritual things. And then how can you stay strong when the enemy tries to attack? You can't."

I paused. I took a deep breath. Then I held firmly to the podium. I now knew what God wanted me to tell them, and they were gonna hear it.

Speaking from my soul, I voiced with passion, "I say to you, my classmates, my friends, people who will forever be a part of my life, as we move from this day, from this moment, from this time, *let God go with you!* Let Jesus

Christ be who you stand for. Guard yourself, so that things of the world can't sway you. I said it before and I'll say it again, I'm proud that I'm finally trying to do things God's way. Why don't you? When you have God, you don't need drugs or alcohol. You can feel good on His love alone. Try it! Try it out there when things get tough. Lean on Him to be your rock. God's best to you all."

I felt an inward peace as I gave them truth. Though I didn't deserve to stand there before them, I was glad God gave me the mission despite my "not so perfect" self. Through all my drama, I could still be real with Him. God did not give up on me. That fact alone was such a blessing, and it was awesome to finally be walking with grace.

Other Titles in the Payton Skky Series

ISBN: 0-8024-4236-6

Staying Pure

Payton Skky has everything a high school senior would want -- popularity, well-to-do parents, and excellent grades. To top that off, she dates the most sought after boy in her school, Dakari Graham. However, when Dakari puts on the pressure to take their relationship to the next level, Payton goes numb. Torn between what her soul believes and what her heart wants, she struggles to make the bestdecision. Will her choice be the right one?

Saved Race

ISBN: 0-8024-4238-2

Payton Skky is about to accomplish a life-long dream- graduate from high school with honors. However, when Payton's gorgeous, biracial, cousin, Pillar Skky steps on the scene and Payton has to deal with feelings of jealousy and anger towards her. Though she knows God wants her to have a tight relationship with her cousin, years of family drama seem to keep them forever apart. Will Payton accept past hurts or embrace God's grace?

Sweetest Gift

Payton Skky now has what she's always longed for - to go to college and live away from home. Though she quickly finds out that being an adult is not easy. When Payton feels her new friends have it goin'on, she begins to lose self-confidence and starts to feel she doesn't fit in. She can't seem to let go of her sad feelings. Can her relationship with Jesus Christ fill her with joy she lacks?

ISBN: 0-8024-4239-0

Surrendered Heart

Payton Skky finally has her priorities straight; to live each moment for God. The legacy of her grandfather's life lets her know that in the end the only thing that will matter is knowing for certain that even though people may reject the message of salvation, she still needs to do her best to represent Christ.

Though she gets discouraged, her good friend Tad Taylor helps to keep her focused on carrying out God's commands. While the two of them try to mend their hearts back together, many things around them fall apart. Will they work out...or will things remain the same?

ISBN: 0-8024-4240-4

MOODY
PUBLISHERS
THE NAME YOU CAN TRUST.

1-800-678-6928 www.MoodyPublishers.com

SOBER FAITH TEAM

ACQUIRING EDITOR:
Cynthia Ballenger

COPY EDITOR:
Chandra Sparks Taylor

COVER DESIGN:
Lydell Jackson

INTERIOR DESIGN:
Ragont Design

PRINTING AND BINDING:
Versa Press Incorporated

The typeface for the text of this book is
Berkeley